"Let go of the branch," Trace told Sonny.

She was precariously hanging off the tree, sure to fall off the mountain at any second. He couldn't be sure which of the two of them was the more amazed when she let go and dropped into his arms. She was pretty he noticed.

As she tried to wriggle lower in his embrace, Trace held her steady and braced himself against the sheer drop. He couldn't bear to put her down.

"Okay you've had your fun. Now put me down."

"Okay." He let go of her. Gasping, she slid along his body. Trace didn't catch her again until her lips reached the point at which he wanted them. Opposite his.

Sonny still couldn't touch the ground. Not that it mattered. With his lips so close to hers, she'd suddenly lost all feeling in her toes. The left side of Sonny's brain informed her she was insane. The right side wondered how it would feel to part her lips beneath his, to fan the sparks he was igniting in an all-consuming fire. Giving thanks she was right-brained, she kissed him.

Trace wondered how he could have played with fire all these years and never before melted as he was doing now. Finally, when he could, he stopped kissing her and set her on the ground.

His legs were shaking, he noted. "How far is it to the bottom of this mountain?" he asked.

Before she could reply, the path crumbled beneath Trace's feet.

Dear Reader,

As we end another winter, let's welcome spring with another marvelous lineup of romantic comedies featuring two very different, yet equally wonderful stories.

Carolyn Greene has written a romantic and moving story of best friends who finally learn to look for love right under their noses. *The Wedding Deception* is an apt title as our hero and heroine enter into their marriage with very different agendas. She wants a baby; he wants her to fall in love with him!

Valerie Kirkwood spins a zany, fast-paced, fast-talking screwball comedy. *Accidentally Yours* has all the classic elements: a wise-talking hero and heroine, the hero's very eccentric family, mistaken identities and a quest for revenge. Just like the hero does, just jump right in and enjoy!

Next month, I'll be telling you all about Let's Celebrate!, a special promotion with a great contest.

So, keeping you in suspense, and with love—and laughter,

Malle Vallik

Malle Vallik
Associate Senior Editor

ACCIDENTALLY YOURS
Valerie Kirkwood

Harlequin Books

TORONTO • NEW YORK • LONDON
AMSTERDAM • PARIS • SYDNEY • HAMBURG
STOCKHOLM • ATHENS • TOKYO • MILAN
MADRID • WARSAW • BUDAPEST • AUCKLAND

ISBN 0-373-44020-0

ACCIDENTALLY YOURS

This edition published by arrangement with Harlequin Books S.A.

® and TM are trademarks of the publisher. Trademarks indicated with ® are registered in the United States Patent and Trademark Office, the Canadian Trade Marks Office and in other countries.

Printed in U.S.A.

A funny thing happened...

The conventional wisdom is that we should take more time to smell the roses. I've always suspected this advice came to us from the makers of allergy medications, and have generally preferred laughter as my antidote to sneezing and wheezing, instead. I suppose that's because my childhood allergies often kept me indoors where, after demonstrating to Mother that dusting—and just about every other form of housework—caused coughing fits worthy of Camille, I'd click on the TV for a dose of those fabulous screwball comedies of the thirties and forties. Zany plots, urbane dialogue and (sigh) a screen filled with Joel McCrea's shoulders. (*The Palm Beach Story*, 1942. Check it out.) How lucky could a congested romance writer-in-training get?

When you consider that these film gems were written against the backdrop of a global depression and war, do you wonder, as I do, what all the current whining is about? That's why I say stop worrying about the roses your nose will never meet! Tune out the talk shows and the women who are addicted to electrolysis. Just throw back your head and laugh. I hope *Accidentally Yours* helps you to do just that.

Gesundheit!

—Valerie Kirkwood

**For Kate,
accidentally—and blessedly—ours.**

1

"NOMBRE VINGT-QUARTRE. Noir. Number twenty-four. Black."

Trace Whittington watched the croupier sweep the last of his chips from the table. "Ah, well," Trace said, turning to the mannequin who stood peering over his right shoulder. A single blond strand escaped her sleek French twist to fall alongside the shimmer of diamonds that cascaded from her earlobe to her bare shoulder. What was her name again? Gabrielle? That was as good a guess as any. In Monte Carlo, all beautiful women were named Gabrielle and each had identically sculpted features because they went to the same plastic surgeons. Cheek implants, Trace had noticed, were the rage this season. "There goes young Trace's operation."

The woman's brows, which looked as though they had been brushed into place hair by hair, puckered. *"Non, mon cher. Comment triste."*

Wagging his head, Trace sighed. "Yes, it is sad, isn't it? Or at least it would be if there *were* a little Trace." Trace had been anticipating the satisfaction that came with pulling the leg of a leggy female. Instead, at the mention of his nonexistent son, he felt a disturbing pang of genuine sadness in the heart he thought he had long ago anesthetized to most real emotions.

Snap out of it, man, he commanded himself. *Don't take yourself so seriously.* As he knew too well, that could be quite painful. Especially when no one else ever regarded

him as anything but the Whittingtons' younger, and there-
fore, superfluous son. Raising the blonde's hand to his lips,
he peered at her with the seriocomic expression he had
perfected. "You wouldn't care to help me correct that mi-
nor oversight, would you?"

As if from a fate worse than death—stretch marks, Trace
presumed—the woman snatched her hand from his. Then,
slowly, a dazzling capped smile broke through her colla-
gen-filled lips. "You zhoke weez Gabrielle."

"Gabrielle?" Gaping, Trace wondered how he had ever
allowed himself to commit the ultimate faux pas—getting
into a rut. Next season, he decided, he'd squander what
Arthur was paying him to stay out of the family's vast
business affairs in some other magic kingdom for the idle
rich. In Corfu, perhaps, where he supposed all beautiful
women were named Mercedes or Olympia.

"Yes, I joke," he said. "The perpetuation of the family
dynasty I leave to Arthur Whittington V, my older brother.
He, after all, has the Whittington nose, which can't get
enough of the paneled-wood scent of the boardroom." A
boardroom that badly needed an airing, Trace thought.
Then he reminded himself that Whittington Enterprises was
no longer his concern, not since he had challenged Arthur
for the chairmanship five years ago and gone down flaming.

Gabrielle dangled her hands over Trace's shoulders, flut-
tering her expensive sable lashes at him as though he was
an entry in the Monte Carlo Rally she was trying to flag to
a stop. *"Quel dommage,"* she whispered as she ran the tip
of her index finger down his own very un-Whittington-like
nose, over his lips, and rested it in the cleft of his chin.
"You really would make such beautiful *bébés.*"

Gratified she had apparently decided there was no reason
to throw the hot-tub water out with the baby, Trace nevertheless couldn't resist another tug on her lovely limb.
"Yes, and so much American manufacturing is going off-
shore these days."

Gabrielle pushed on Trace's diamond-studded shirtfront. "Weez the right woman, *naturellement.*"

"Of course, naturally." Releasing her, Trace assumed an academic air. "Nine times out of ten, I prefer that method to—"

Throwing back her head, Gabrielle laughed like crystal chimes in the wind as she shimmied her shoulders once, prettily. "I think you are a man who eez never *serieux.*"

"*Faites les paris,*" the croupier called. "Make your bets."

Trace rose. "I assure you, Gabrielle, when it comes to losing money at roulette, I can be very serious. *Venez avec moi.*"

Taking her by the elbow, Trace guided Gabrielle through the throng of high-stakes gamblers, halting her beside a bronze male nude that reminded him of what he was likely to be left with if he didn't win back some of the small fortune he'd dropped that night. "Darling Gabrielle, now that we understand each other—" seeing foreplay and a promise not to ask for promises in her eyes, Trace had no doubt they did "—I want nothing more than to make this a night to remember. But first I must pay a visit to my old friend, Michel." Crooking his finger, he lifted the blonde du jour's lovely implanted chin. "Will you wait for me?"

Leaning past Trace, Gabrielle glinted greedily at the cashier's cage. "*A l'éternité,*" she said, her mouth forming a glistening pout.

Trace molded his lips to it, then broke into a grin. "Well, for as long as I can afford to remain in this overgrown playpen, anyway, *n'est-ce pas?*"

Noting Gabrielle's smile, which to her credit was both coy and shameless, Trace flicked the tip of her nose and strode to the cashier's window. "More of those little round things, Michel. *Toute de suite.*"

"*Mais,* Monsieur Whittington—"

"I know, I know," Trace said, holding up his hands in

protest. "But there's really no need to thank me for continuing to favor the casino with my losses. Let's just say I'm sentimental about the place, though I do think the least the management could do is to name one of the rooms after me."

"Monsieur—"

"All right. I'm a reasonable man. A small plaque inscribed with my name on one of the craps tables, then."

"Monsieur Whittington, *je regret*—"

"You can't be any sorrier than I am, Michel." Trace motioned the cashier closer. "What would you say to a moment of silence on my birthday?"

"Monsieur!"

Trace laughed, then cast a glance at Gabrielle, who ran her tongue over her lips.

"Look Michel," Trace said, tapping a series of staccatos on the sill of the cage. "Don't advance me too much. Just enough to ensure I recover a token of my losses and all of my sparkling wit. I think both are going to come in handy tonight."

"Again, Monsieur Whittington, I am very sorry—"

"Yes, yes, so you've said." With a sidelong look at Gabrielle, Trace tugged on the ends of the black-and-white Escher bow tie that matched the vest of his tuxedo. "*Vite*, Michel, the chips. I believe my luck has changed."

"It certainly has, Monsieur."

Trace may have read nothing in the *Wall Street Journal* for the last five years but the arts page and ads for villa rentals, but he knew the sound of pleasure turning into business when he heard it. "What are you talking about?"

"I regret to inform Monsieur that I cannot increase his limit."

Trace squared his shoulders. "And Monsieur is certain there must be some mistake."

"There is no mistake, Monsieur Whittington."

Trace ground his jaw to one side. "Tell René I wish to see him."

"He is expecting you, Monsieur," the cashier replied, indicating the office of the casino's manager. "Please go in."

Turning to Gabrielle, Trace held up his index finger to signal that he would return before her silicone cooled. His charm must be in better shape than René's books because the kiss she blew him caused every man who saw it to stop and regard him with such admiration he thought they were going to salute. With a wink at Gabrielle that was somewhere between "I'm going to take you to paradise" and "I'm going to take you home to Mother," Trace burst into René Broussard's office.

"René, what's this business about the casino not being able to up my limit? Or are you afraid that if I keep losing, the place will look like the clip joint that it is?"

A fiftyish man of medium build, elegant in a double-breasted tuxedo, rose from behind a Louis Quinze desk and, with a broad sincere smile, extended his hand to Trace. "So good to see you again, Monsieur. The last time we met, as I recall, you were with your lovely sister and her new husband. How is she?"

"Divorced."

"I'm sorry to hear that."

"It's all right. I just heard she's married the court stenographer."

Broussard's brows arched. "I see."

"Do you? Because I'm damned if I do," Trace replied as he shook the man's hand. "It was one of those professional relationships that suddenly blossoms into romance, I suppose. Bob recorded all her divorce trials."

"Bob?"

Frowning, Trace shoved his hands into his pockets. "You're right, he was the second husband. Maybe this one is Brad. No, he was the gardener Bob never should have hired. Anyway,'' he said, going to the far wall to study the framed sketches lining it, ''if you'll just take a moment to discover where in my accounts you misplaced that decimal point, I'll be on my way.''

''There has been no misplaced decimal point, Monsieur.''

As if reacting to a blow, Trace's eyes narrowed on the signature in the lower right corner of one of the sketches. *Matisse.* They were all Matisses. Calculating how many of them his losses had purchased, he turned to René Broussard. ''I've been a patron of your tables for the last five years, René. Has my brother ever once failed to make good on my debts?''

Broussard shook his head. ''*Non, c'est vrai.* He has not.''

Trace emitted an incredulous laugh. ''Then what's the problem?''

Walking to his desk, Broussard opened a drawer and removed a magazine. ''This,'' he said, handing the glossy to Trace, who glanced at the cover, then smiled at Broussard as if he'd caught him reading *Penthouse.*

''*Célébrité?* I'm surprised at you, René.'' Trace shoved the magazine back at Broussard's midsection. ''*Celebrity* is nothing more than the social register's version of *People.*''

''Perhaps,'' Broussard said, though rather than accepting the magazine, he withdrew a silver case from his inside breast pocket. Opening it, he offered a cigarette to Trace. When Trace declined, he lit one for himself, then exhaling, said, ''Still, I think you should read the article on page *quarante-huit.* Forty—''

''Eight. Thanks, but I think I'll pass.''

Holding his cigarette between his thumb and middle finger, and narrowing his eyes on Trace, Broussard took a drag. ''I'm afraid that's all you will be doing in Monte Carlo for a while, Monsieur.''

Trace raised an eyebrow, then planting his fists on his

waist, smiled. "You had me going for a moment, René. But your Inspector Clousseau impersonation gave you away." He dropped the society scandal sheet on the desk. "It's been a blast. Now please tell Michel to have my playthings ready."

As Trace turned toward the door, Broussard clamped a hand on his shoulder. When Trace looked over that same shoulder, there was *Celebrity,* in his face. "*Zut,* René, but you're getting to be a bore," he said, then stepped around Broussard and away from the magazine. "Whatever it is you think you've latched on to, you know you can't believe everything you read in that rag."

"Not everything, Monsieur," René said, turning and stepping toward Trace. "Just what the Baroness Oleska writes."

When his eyes returned to their normal size, Trace shoved his hands into his pockets again, threw back his head, and gave a belly laugh.

"Perhaps Monsieur would care to share the source of his amusement," Broussard said, sounding as though he had just sampled an insolent Bordeaux.

"I'm sorry, René," Trace replied, containing his mirth as he perched on the corner of the desk. "It's just that I never cease to be amazed at the power of a title over here, even a phony one. You don't really believe there actually is a Baroness Oleska, do you?"

Broussard sniffed. "It is an old and respected name on the continent."

Leaning forward, Trace crossed his hands on his thigh. "Well, now it's an old and not-too-respected pen name for a bottom-dwelling reporter."

"You know this? You have met the baroness?"

"No, but a dog doesn't have to have been introduced to a tick to know it's there." Following the lead of his raised hackles, Trace straightened. "The 'baroness' has sucked Whittington blood before."

Taking two steps forward, Broussard persisted in offering Trace the magazine. "Then I'm afraid she is doing it again, Monsieur."

This time, hearing an ominous sobriety in René's tone, Trace took the latest issue of *Celebrity*. As he flipped through the pages, he recalled a whiff he once caught driving past a sewage plant. It was a high-tech, multimillion-dollar sewage plant, but it still reeked. Almost as bad as the caption of an item on page forty-eight. Silently, he translated back into English from the French translation, then looked at Broussard, his gaze a black hole. Standing, he threw the magazine down on the desk, then stalked behind the letter. "'Will the Witless Whittingtons Be Left without a Whit?'! What the hell is that supposed to mean?"

Broussard stubbed his cigarette in the ashtray on his desk. "Your older brother, Arthur, is the chairman and CEO of Whittington Enterprises, *non?*"

"He was groomed for the job like the Prince of Wales and he's welcome to it," Trace said, disturbed that after five years he could still detect a false note in his avowal that he hadn't the least interest in running Whittington, Inc. "What of it?"

"According to the baroness, he's made some—how shall I put it?—rather unfortunate investments."

"They can't have been as unfortunate as mine were tonight." Trace laughed, inviting Broussard to join in. But the man only pursed his thin lips more tightly.

"You may not find it so amusing when I tell you the markets are very concerned, Monsieur."

Trace straightened his spine, trying to fend off concerns of his own. Then, recalling the source of Broussard's information, he relaxed. "What tripe," he said. "Even by *Celebrity*'s standards, which is probably an oxymoron."

Shrugging, Broussard made a tsking sound. "Monsieur Whittington, personally, I like you. And this whole business is most unpleasant for me. But I have spoken to the editor and he stands by the baroness's story."

Trace couldn't remember the last time he felt anger, one of those emotions he had ceased to feel when he had ceased to much care what became of him. But what was boiling inside him now came close. Either that, or he was doing a pretty good imitation of his cappuccino maker. "You did *what?*"

"Monsieur, a casino is a business—"

"Fine!" Raking back the thick comma of hair that had tumbled onto his forehead, Trace headed for the door, pausing to point a finger at Broussard. "But I'm certain there are casinos in Monte Carlo whose management does not consult *Celebrity* magazine when checking their patrons' credit."

As he reached the door, Trace heard Broussard address him by his first name, something the older man with the even older old-world formality had never done before. He halted, but did not turn around.

"You would do me a great honor, Trace, by saving yourself further embarrassment," Broussard said softly. "Perhaps, as you say, it isn't true that Arthur Whittington has been unable to raise the capital he needs to prop up his holdings. But the news is all over Monte Carlo, and I suspect elsewhere by now."

Broussard, Trace knew, was right. One thing that flowed more freely on the Riviera than suntan oil was gossip. He opened the door, admitting the din of fortunes being lost and won, and lost again. Then he turned, forcing himself to smile as he pointed at the wall behind Broussard. "Take care of those Matisses, René. If the baroness shows up, you can show her proof that not all of the Whittington investments have been unfortunate."

Closing the door behind him, Trace directed his gaze to the bronze nude, now deserted, and laughed to himself, or maybe it was at himself. So Gabrielle would wait for him till eternity, was it? *C'est la vie* and just as well, he supposed, slipping his hands into his very empty pockets. One thing he didn't doubt, however, was that thanks to that muckraking phony at *Celebrity,* he was now persona non grata at every casino in Monte. He'd not only lost the ability to recoup his stakes, but his sense of humor, as well.

But only temporarily. He'd return to Palm Beach, where he'd see to it that in a contest with the Baroness Oleska, he'd have the last laugh. First, though, he had to call his lawyer.

HEARING THE PHONE CHIRP, Sonny Chapin blindly turned off the shower, knocking the shampoo bottle from the caddie and spilling the contents on her feet. As dollops of henna-highlights-for-brunettes lather slid down her forehead and over her tightly shut eyes, she turned toward the back wall, groping for the towel she knew hung there. Unable to reach it, she took a step closer and instantly felt her soles slide in the opposite direction. Fortunately she lunged in reaction and latched onto the sides of the towel. Unfortunately the cheap plastic towel bar came crashing down and Sonny slid into the tub like an oyster from its shell. Lying on her belly with the towel over her head, she grabbed the portable phone sitting on the vanity chair outside the curtain as though nothing out of the ordinary had just occurred—which, for Sonny Chapin, was indeed the case.

"Hello?"

"Congratulations, Baroness."

Sonny got to her knees, draping the towel around her neck and wiping her eyes with one corner of it. "Jack?"

"I just heard your little item on the Whittingtons has flushed their young scion out of the gambling dens of Monte Carlo. He arrived in Palm Beach last night."

At the sound of her editor's raspy baritone and the news it brought, Sonny sat back, hugging her knees with her free arm and smiling crookedly. "Aw, what happened? Did all the cruel heartless casinos take away his toys and kick him out of the great big sandbox?"

"With the pointy toes of their Ferragamos."

Sonny began scrubbing the back of her head, breaking a nail. "And all because of my little ol' column?" she asked.

"Probably, but don't let it go to your unfathomable but adorable auburn head."

"No time for that," she said, squinting at her waterproof watch. "There's a flight leaving Kennedy for Palm Beach International in a few hours. If I hurry I can make it. Maybe now the elusive Mr. Trace Whittington will deign to talk to me."

"Nix, Sonny."

Thinking she hadn't heard Jack correctly, Sonny adjusted the receiver at her ear. "Say again?" she asked, picking at the broken fingernail.

"I don't want you going anywhere near the guy," Jack replied. "Last night he told the press—"

"The press?" Sonny's journalistic instincts perked. If Trace Whittington had finally met with reporters, he'd undoubtedly faced photographers, too—something he'd managed to avoid since his graduation from an Eastern prep school. Judging from that picture, she didn't blame him. When, exactly, he'd gone from geeky to reputedly gorgeous, she had no way of knowing. Of course, for anyone fascinated by the back of his head, the back of his hand, or the back of his Armani jacket as he shielded his face from the camera, an entire *oeuvre* existed. There was even a snapshot of him having breakfast with an international supermodel in Capri—and of the palm frond hiding all but his dark glasses. The incredible truth was that not even the most ingenious paparazzi had been able to capture a recent, identifiable close-up of one of the world's most eligible— and publicity-hating—bachelors. Until now.

"Jack," Sonny began, her heart close to pounding,

"don't tell me we're finally going to get a gander at the face that launched a thousand divorces?"

"Okay, I won't."

Sonny blinked. "You won't?"

"Sorry," Jack replied. "But you're going to have to keep imagining what Casanova Whittington looks like." He explained that Trace hadn't actually met with the press last night. He'd only called the wire services from the Whittington estate. "He said your story was irresponsible and he intended to hold you and the magazine accountable for personal financial loss, as well as for any damages the adverse publicity might have caused the Whittington holdings."

"*Me* irresponsible?" Doubly irritated, first by Trace Whittington's continued elusiveness and second by his accusation, Sonny thrust her legs out in front of her. As she did, she slid backward and had to grab the soap dish to keep from being speared in the back by the faucet. "My source for the Whittington stories is reliable, Jack, which is more than anyone can say about Trace Whittington."

"Your source is a leak close to the Whittingtons who calls herself Madame X and communicates with you only when the moon is full. By private messenger."

"She can communicate with me by messenger pigeon for all I care," Sonny shot back. "She hasn't been wrong yet, has she?"

Jack was silent for a moment. "Sonny," he said, "it's more than a matter of accuracy. For some reason you've gone out of your way to make the Whittingtons look like a separate category under the heading 'Cognitively Challenged.'"

"I didn't have to go very far out of my way." Pushing the curtain aside, Sonny leaned over the edge of the tub and removed a strawberry-licorice twist from the bag on the chair. "What about the father, Arthur Four? How many people do you know who fund an organization that claims it can trace your ancestry to Mars?''

"All right, " Jack said, his sigh audible. "I'll admit the Interplanetary Genealogical Society isn't the American Heart Association—''

"It isn't even Save the Spotted Owl, Jack.''

"Who gives a hoot?''

Sonny rolled her eyes.

"Sorry," Jack said. "But so what if old Arthur Whittington thinks we all came from outer space? The longer I stay in this job the more I think he may be on to something.''

Making a face as if to concede Jack had a point, Sonny bit a section of licorice from the twist. "What about Mrs. Whittington?''

"A lot of people paint for a hobby, Sonny.''

"Houses?'' Brandishing her arm, Sonny's jaw dropped as she watched what was left of her licorice sail out of her slippery fingers, hit the steamed mirror across the room and drop into the sink. She turned and propped her back against the tub, then raised her feet to the tile wall in front of her. "I mean, when we're talking oils here, we're talking Sherwin Williams.''

"Some women like a .44 Magnum," Jack said, his tone suggesting a shrug. "She likes a spray gun. Anything else?''

As her feet slid involuntarily up the wall, Sonny's bottom shifted and the back of her head hit the edge of the tub. She lay there, gazing up at the burned-out bulb in the ceiling. "Yeah. The daughter. Diana DimWhittington? When she filed for a divorce from Jordan Kent, she was stunned to find out she'd never married him. According to Madame X, Diana said, 'I never did have a mind for details.' If you ask me, she never had a mind.''

"So who the hell asked you?!''

Sonny held the phone away from her ear. It wasn't like

Jack Conroy to shout. It was less like him to censor her, especially when it came to the peccadilloes of the rich and fatuous. "What's wrong, Jack?"

There was a long silence, then Jack said, "Look, I just think we ought to lay off the Whittingtons for a while."

"Lay *off?*" Sonny sat up, draping the towel over the side of the tub and anchoring her arm over it. "Jack, you said yourself they sell almost as many magazines as Princess Di."

"Exactly. And if all the king's horses and all the king's men can't put Humpty Whittington, Inc. together again, I don't want Trace Whittington blaming us. I don't want a libel suit on my hands, Sonny."

"Neither do I, Jack. But we're not talking rumors here."

"I don't care. I want you to ease off, do you hear me?"

Glancing down at the floor, Sonny noticed her slipper. Lifting it, she poured out the puddle of water it had collected from the towel dripping above it. "Is this you or the magazine's legal paranoiacs talking?"

"Both."

Suddenly terribly cold, she put down the slipper and wrapped her arm about her. "All right, if that's your final decision. But I can't believe you of all people is wimping out."

"Maybe I'm not wimping out, Sonny," Jack replied. "Maybe you're burning out."

"What's that supposed to mean?" Sonny waited. "Jack?"

"You know I think you're a terrific writer, Sonny, but lately your copy's been…"

"Been what, Jack? Say it!"

"Okay." His tone was as dry as she was wet. "It's been petty and vindictive. Especially your pieces on the Whittingtons. It's starting to look like a vendetta, kid."

"Vendetta? Why would I—"

"I don't know. You tell me."

Sonny examined the scar on her palm that ran lengthwise from between the first and second fingers of her right hand to the base of her thumb. After ten years it had faded to a thin white line, but the memory of how her father had reacted to her getting her hand caught in one of his factory's machines was still vivid. First he had scolded her for leaving the university and sneaking into the plant against his long-standing order that she stay away from the equipment. Then, after she'd been stitched and he'd seen she was all right, he had kissed her and said, "When you give a fella a hand, you don't fool around." Even now, Sonny smiled at the memory of him thanking her for pitching in to save his most important customer and so many jobs. He had told her he was proud of her for not thinking factory work was beneath the boss's daughter and for realizing the importance of everyone pulling together to make a business a success. Finally, raising her small bandaged hand gently with his big one—one that bore scars and calluses of its own—he had brought his lips to it in that courtly manner of his. Then, telling her she could do more good wielding her pen than running a crimp machine, he had driven her back to Northwestern, where she majored in journalism.

Years later, after a disappointing string of stints on small-city newspapers, never breaking that one story that would catalyze her career, she had failed to do much good. But at least she was in a position now to exact sweet revenge for what Whittington, Inc. had done to the once thriving business her father had built over a lifetime. If she wanted to hang on to that position, she had to allay Jack's suspicions.

Crawling over the edge of the tub like a soldier over a wall, she walked to the cabinet over the commode and pulled down a fresh towel. "Look, Jack," she said, scrunching her face as a roll of toilet paper tumbled to its destiny. "People like the Whittingtons give me a large pain, that's all."

"Me, too, Sonny. But I don't make the mistake of underestimating them. Especially Trace."

"He's the worst of the lot." As though she had just seen something reptilian, Sonny shivered. "He's the only one who has the brains and talent to manage the company, but he's too busy doing a bad imitation of Cary Grant in *An Affair to Remember* to notice that if Whittington, Inc. goes down, thousands of jobs go down with it."

"Cut the guy some slack, Sonny," Jack replied. "You know he tried to take over the chairmanship once and was shot down."

"That's exactly what I mean. He tried *once*."

"His father and his sister split their share votes between him and Arthur, but the other directors did what directors get paid to do. They sided with the powers that be." Jack gave a laugh. "The man never stood a chance."

"So—" Sonny tucked the phone beneath her chin and wrapped the towel around her "—was that any reason to take a payoff from his brother and run away with his tail between his legs?"

"Yes! I'm surprised the man didn't say, 'You won't have Trace Whittington to kick around anymore,' while he was at it." Sonny could hear Jack gulp coffee she knew he'd probably reheated from the night before. "Look, at least give him credit for bucking a tradition that's over a hundred years old. Nobody named anything but Arthur has ever run Whittington Enterprises."

"And what if one of the Arthurs has daughters instead of sons?"

"Then it's *Morte d'Artur,* I guess," Jack said, laughing. "Seriously, they'd probably just rename the oldest girl Arthur. That's how entrenched they are in the tradition of handing the operation of the company down to the firstborn of the firstborn."

Sonny began squeezing the excess water from her hair. "If that's Trace's only excuse for copping out, Jack, I'm not buying it. He isn't just some—'' Suddenly she felt her towel come undone. Lurching to retrieve it, she lost her chin grip on the phone, which crashed to the hard tile and skidded away from her.

"Sonny? Sonny? You still there?"

"I'm here, Jack," she shouted, pursuing the phone, which began to resemble a frog trying to evade capture. When she finally got hold of it, she plunked down on her forearms, her bare fanny in the air. She exhaled a breath. "As I was saying, Trace Whittington isn't just some victim of birth order. My father was lost in the middle of a pack of nine kids, yet he—"

"Oh-h-h, I get it," Jack said.

Hearing his chair creak, Sonny could just see him leaning back, propping his ankle on his knee and looking superior. She hated it when he looked superior, which he did frequently. It was only one of the reasons she had ended their romantic involvement. "Get what?" she asked, emphasizing each word.

"You know, Sonny, for the first time I feel sorry for Trace Whittington."

She snorted. "Doesn't everyone?"

"No, I mean it."

"Why would you ever feel sorry for him, Jack?"

"Because no man can survive comparison to Saint Edward Chapin, that's why," Jack replied. "And I ought to know."

Sonny fell silent. They'd had this conversation before, apparently to no avail. Sure, she idolized her father, and why shouldn't she? Edward Chapin was an honorable and compassionate man, a man of conscience. The kind of man who wasn't exactly running rampant on the streets of New York. But it certainly wasn't his giant shadow that had cast a pall over her romance with Jack. Jack just hadn't been the one. He wasn't the man she dreamed of one day falling—and falling hard—for. When she did, there'd be no doubts, no second thoughts, and until that moment, no shared accommodations just because she was getting tired of eating alone in front of the TV. She needed more than the sight of a man's razor and shaving cream in her medicine cabinet to make her happy. She wanted to respect the man she would eventually commit to, so much so she'd be willing to fight his battles with him. That was the way her mother had felt about her father and he about her. The way she and Jack were never going to feel about each other.

Sonny got to her feet. "Listen, Jack, you caught me in the shower and I'm all soapy and—"

"Sure you don't need me to scrub your back?"

"Jack, don't."

"Cancel that," he said. "I forgot. You don't need any man."

"That's not true."

"Okay, I take it back."

"Thank you."

"You do need your casualty-insurance agent."

"How droll," Sonny retorted, then promptly walked into the metal leg of the vanity chair, sending it crashing against the tub.

"What was *that?*"

Massaging her throbbing toes, her eyes stinging, Sonny hopped on one foot and tried to regain her breath. "Nothing," she squeezed out. "I'll see you at the office, Jack, okay?"

"No, it's not okay."

Suddenly feeling her breath return, Sonny put her smarting foot down. *"What?"*

"You and the Baroness Oleska are now on leave until further notice," Jack said. "You've both earned time off. Go to Disney World, go visit your father on that holy mountaintop of his in North Carolina—"

"Go fly a kite is what you mean! You want me out of

town before Trace Whittington slaps me with a summons."
Damn. "Is that an order, Jack?"

"Don't forget to send a postcard," Jack said, then hung
up.

Temporarily coerced out of her job, Sonny not only
added one more count to her list of indictments against
Trace Whittington, she decided to throw the book at him
once and for all. He was nothing, she knew, if not a gam-
bler. But if he was going to roll the litigation dice against
her, he'd have to put more than money on the line. He'd
have to bet his jet-set life.

2

IN LOW-SLUNG WHITE SHORTS, shirtless and barefoot, Trace stepped through an arch in the loggia that overlooked the Atlantic and the pool on the grounds of the Whittington estate. Instantly he fell back, shielding his eyes. After a week of gambling nights and sleeping days, he'd become a stranger to natural light, much less the blazing South Florida sun at high noon.

"Coffee, dear?"

Peering through the Italian sunglasses he had just lowered from the top of his head, Trace glimpsed the woman who had addressed him from the poolside gazebo. She was dressed in overalls and a T-shirt and wore a red bandanna on her head. "Make it a double, Mom."

Lotti Whittington lifted the coffee carafe. "Jet lag?"

Trace sat across from his mother and gazed at the pool, glistening like a cache of aquamarines in the sun. A treasure, he discovered last night, he had too long taken for granted. "I'm not the one who's lagging, Lotti Mae," he said, taking the cup she handed him.

"I assume that remark was intended for me." Arthur Whittington V, kissing his mother on the cheek, sat between her and his brother and helped himself to a cup of coffee.

Leaning back, Trace hooked one leg over the arm of the chair. "For once your timing is impeccable, Artie."

"How many times must I ask you not to address me by that name, Trace?" Arthur flapped his napkin onto his lap.

"And how can you come to the table looking like that? As usual, it appears, you haven't shaved in a week."

Interrupting a sip from his cup, Trace rasped the backs of his fingers across his cheek and grinned. "If you think my stubble drives *you* crazy, you should see what it does to women."

Inhaling so deeply his nostrils became pinched, Arthur turned to Lotti. "Mother, I don't see how you can tolerate—"

"Please, boys," Lotti said. "Let's not have another scene like last night's. Your father was so upset he went off to the observatory and hasn't come out since."

"Tell, *him!*" Arthur thrust a finger at his brother, who feigned shock. "He's the one who dared to accuse us of serving ourselves on a platter to the press, as if his amorous escapades haven't provided every bit as much fodder."

Abruptly sitting forward, Trace set his cup down with a rattle. "Look, Artie, my escapades, as you call them, don't affect Whittington stock." He ground his teeth against the renewed urge to hang Arthur by his Brooks Brothers tie. He would have done so last night when he learned that the Baroness Oleska's story about Arthur's blunders as the head of Whittington, Inc. had been no exaggeration. Now, as then, only the thought of a double hanging, with the baroness swinging beside Arthur, prevented him. "I'm not the one who's running Whittington into the ground. I'm not even a voting member of the board anymore, remember?"

"Which you agreed to."

Trace said nothing. The truth was, he *had* taken the money and run. Moreover, he'd convinced himself he'd been smart to bail out before Arthur put the company on the shoals as he had once predicted. But the temptation to gloat withered at the appearance of a stronger sensation that, if memory served him correctly, was a pang of conscience. An inconvenient pang, too, considering he had grown accustomed to being paid handsomely not to exercise his conscience.

"Besides," Arthur added, "for all the fight you put up to strip me of my birthright, you wouldn't have lasted six months as chairman of Whittington. The way you've been living proves you're allergic to responsibility."

Rocketing to his feet, his fists clenched, Trace glared down at his brother. *Damn you to hell, Arthur.* He was daring Trace to say what he was thinking. When A.W. had had double pneumonia and the doctors weren't sure he'd make it, it wasn't Arthur who barely left their father's bedside, not Arthur who torqued his back sleeping in a chair. And when Lotti had undergone a mastectomy, Arthur hadn't been the one who pushed a paint roller around under her supervision, keeping her spirits up until she recovered enough to paint again herself. *But you know I won't say these things, don't you, Arthur? You know that if I did I'd be violating what little code of decency I have left.* A decent man didn't justify himself with the willing sacrifices he'd made and would have made again in a heartbeat. But he didn't let a SOB like Arthur—or the Shrewess Oleska—get away with labeling him irresponsible, either.

"What I'm allergic to," he said, his voice hard-edged, "is the dust of outmoded thinking you're burying Whittington, Inc. under."

Arthur pinched the bridge of his narrow nose. "I refuse to waste my time listening to you harangue about bringing the corporation into the twenty-first century and other such nonsense." Then, slashing a look at Trace, he added, "For the last time let me remind you that you gave up your right to have a say a long time ago."

And we both know what will happen to me if I try to get it back, don't we, Artie? Hell, everyone knew, even that harpy, the baroness. Arthur would cut off his support, right down to the last franc, ruble, yen and lira. He was probably the only corporate director in the world being paid *not* to serve on the board. But not everyone knew about the additional agreement he had signed in a self-spiting moment of despair, the one that staked his inheritance trust fund against Arthur's chairmanship. If Trace attempted another takeover and lost, he'd be left so destitute the IRS would hold a fund-raiser for him and call it Tax Aid.

Casting his brother a sidelong smile that was half contemptuous and half wondrous of his cold-bloodedness, Trace said, "You don't need to remind me, Artie. And don't worry, giving up my say wasn't as big a sacrifice as you think."

"Oh?"

Trace saw Arthur's brows arch as if to ask what could be worse than sacrificing twenty million dollars. "A say isn't worth much if nobody's listening."

With some satisfaction, Trace noted that Arthur was clearly perplexed. In his brother's mind, the worth of a thing and its monetary value were one and the same. Take the pool, for example, he thought as he stepped to its edge, sat down and plunged his feet into the warm clear water. Arthur couldn't count as part of its worth the memories it now brought back to Trace, who had been the only one of the three Whittington offspring to enjoy it in childhood. Arthur had always disdained anything remotely like fun, while Diana had maintained an arsenal of bikinis intended more for capturing male attention than for swimming.

But for Trace, the sight of the pool conjured the sounds of water splashing and slogging against its sides in the middle of a starry night. Sounds he used to lie awake hoping to hear, signaling that his father had left the observatory and dived in. Having worn his trunks to bed, he'd throw back the covers and bolt downstairs. Without stopping for a breath, he'd jump into the pool and try to keep pace with A.W.'s laps. Trace didn't recall they talked much afterward if at all, but he still liked to think those secret swims had meant as much to his father as they had to him.

Lord, but that was a long time ago, and so much had changed since. No, everything had changed. A.W. had retired after thirty years of solid leadership of Whittington Enterprises, Inc. modernizing it not as much as he would have liked but as much as he was able, considering a board whose members fondly recalled Calvin Coolidge. Now Arthur was doing his best to reverse what growth and innovation A.W. had managed to achieve. And there wasn't a damn thing Trace could do to stop him without risking abject poverty, which for some reason, held less than dazzling appeal for him. Still, Whittington was in trouble, and for the first time in five years, he was aware that he had no idea where its stock was priced. Suddenly he wanted to know. Planting his feet on the terrazzo, he leaned back on his forearms, striking a practiced pose of casual indifference. "I hope it's okay for me to ask what the word is on The Street this morning?"

"Our stock opened slightly higher, if that's what you mean," Arthur said, his smile both smug and dismissive. "Undoubtedly on the news of our upcoming meeting on debt restructuring."

"Artie, Artie, Artie." Trace turned on his side and propped his head in his hand, deciding that ceding a stake in the company didn't mean he couldn't be a thorn in his brother's side. "You're going to have to restructure a lot more than your debt. I know you don't want to hear it, but this *is* the '90s, bro. The *19*90s. You know, cyberspace, international trade. Running lean and mean—"

"Mother," Arthur said, making a show of forbearance as he turned to Lotti, "if you don't want a repetition of last evening's brouhaha, you're going to have to take a stand."

"Oh, I hate having to choose," Lotti said. "Which do you think, Arthur? Celestial Rose or Sunset Mauve?"

Arthur backed away from the two paint-sample cards Lotti thrust in his face as if they were his junk bonds come due. "Really, Mother."

"Which do you think the solarium would look best in, Trace?" Walking to the pool, Lotti squatted beside her younger son.

Trace peered at the colored strips. "Celestial Rose has a certain *piquant* quality." He gave his mother an indulgent grin. "On the other hand, Lotti, it reminds me of peppermint ice cream."

"Hmm, yes. I see your point. Too sweet," Lotti replied. "You don't think the mauve is too mauvy?"

Trace sat up, inclining his head toward his mother's, and studied the strip she held up to catch the light. "Well, maybe a little. How about Luscious Lilac?"

"Oh, for heaven's sake!" Arthur pushed away from the table. "If you two will excuse me, I have some rather important work to do, like making sure you have walls to paint, Mother."

"Good morning, darlings!"

Trace, Lotti and Arthur turned in unison toward the voice chiming at the far end of the terrace.

"Diana, you're just in time," Arthur said, flinging his napkin onto the table. "You can help Trace and Mother with a terribly weighty decision regarding the color of the solarium."

"Now, Arthur," Diana soothed, patting down her brother's striped tie, then slipping her arm through his. "You know, you two boys kept me up all night. I lose my center when you fight and call each other nasty-wasty names."

Rising, Trace helped his mother to her feet, then walked over to his sister. He bent to kiss her on the top of her currently red head. "I don't know, Dee, you look pretty centered to me. Don't you think Dee looks centered, Artie?"

"Oh my, yes," Arthur replied, his blue eyes icy behind wire-rimmed glasses. "And I'm sure our creditors will be most reassured to know Dee is centered."

"No wonder you're having problems, Arthur," Dee remarked. "Just look at the negative energy you release. It's nothing less than cosmic pollution."

"Arthur's trouble isn't negative energy, Diana," Lotti said, studying a third paint sample she lifted from the table as she sat down. "It's negative cash flow."

"And negative publicity," Trace added, dropping onto

a nearby chaise. "Let's not forget that someone high up in the Whittington organization is leaking to that scavenging Baroness Oleska."

"Actually that's why I'm here," Diana said, circling her gaze. "I think I have a solution to our problem."

Taking her by the shoulders, Arthur turned his sister toward him. "You've taken my advice to divorce that penniless scribe and marry Hayden Asterbrook. Diana, you don't know what this means to me." He shoved his hands into his pockets and puffed out his chest. "Having an Asterbrook on the board is just what we need to instill confidence in our creditors and the markets."

Diana stepped back, flattening her hand over her heart. "Arthur, don't be ridiculous! Brian and I haven't even unpacked from our honeymoon yet."

"Brian, of course," Trace said, snapping his fingers.

"Besides," Dee continued, her voice softening, "for the first time in my life, I know what it is to really love someone and be loved in return. I'll never leave Brian, even if it means losing my inheritance."

Trace's brows shot up. "This one I have to meet," he muttered.

Arthur slumped into his chair and, folding his arms, went into a sulk. "That's fine for you to say, Diana, but what about the rest of us? What about me? After all, Lydia and I have a certain standing in the community to maintain and three children to put through Harvard."

"I _am_ thinking of you, Arthur. Of the whole family," Diana replied. "When I mentioned I had a solution to our problem, I was referring to those columns the baroness wrote about us."

"Columns?" Lifting his dark glasses, Trace gave his sister a querulous look. "They were serial murders, you mean."

"Oh, I don't know about that," Arthur said, peering around Diana at his brother. "I thought what she had to say about you was actually quite amusing. What was it she wrote: 'Women of St. Tropez, on guard. Trace, or should the baroness say "Without-A-Trace Whittington" is jetting your way.'"

"Ah-ah-ah, Artie," Trace cautioned, dropping his glasses over his eyes and propping his hands behind his head. "Or should I refer to the CEO of Whittington Enterprises as the 'Czar of Ego and Obsolescence'?"

Arthur jumped to his feet. "You take that back!"

"The baroness is the one who has to take it back, Artie," Trace said. "Don't worry, I've already instructed our attorneys to file suit for libel."

"Oh, Trace, you didn't!" Diana plunked herself down on the chaise at her brother's feet.

Removing his glasses, Trace stared at her. "Oh, but I did, big sister. Why else do you think I came back from Monte?" *Other than not being able to get enough credit to play so much as the slot machines, thanks to the baroness.*

Diana fixed Trace with an earnest gaze. "But you *know* violence, so to speak, begets violence."

"Right," Trace replied. He wiggled his fingers as if he was typing. "The baroness begot us with a poison Apple, and I'm begetting her back." Seeing that his computer-illiterate sister clearly did not apprehend his pun and that she was "grieving for the universe," as she would put it, he said, "All right, Dee, tell us exactly what nonviolence you have planned. How do you intend to stop that hack from getting us laughed right out of the *Fortune 500*."

Breaking into a beatific smile Trace found both incongruous—considering Dee's less than saintly life—and irresistible, she said, "Since no conflict can be truly resolved unless all parties take responsibility for their part in it, I've meditated on what we've done to cause this Oleska person to write so unlovingly about us."

"I think I'm about to become seriously infirm," Arthur said, clamping his hand to his abdomen and turning away from his family.

Diana followed him, "In a way, it is our own fault, Arthur. After all, I have been married three times—well, four, counting Brian—and Mother does spend a fortune on drop cloths—"

"Get to the point, will you, Diana?" Arthur rounded on her, tapping his wristwatch.

"All right. The point is—" Stretching out her arms, Diana made a sweep of her audience, as if warning everyone to brace themselves to behold her genius. "I thought if we invited the Baroness Oleska down here to spend a week with us, you know, connect with our true inner selves, then she'd write kinder stories and Arthur would get the money he needs and Trace could go back to Monte and..." Smiling as though she expected bouquets of praise, Diana looked at each of her kin.

"Yes, well." Arthur cleared his throat. "As I said, I have work to do."

"And as I said, suit is being filed today." Trace rose, stretched and, putting his sunglasses on, gazed out at the white-capped ocean. "Think I'll go for a sail."

"Arthur! Trace! Don't either of you dare leave." Diana came to Trace's side. "I certainly thought you would have seen the healing power in my idea."

Trace wrapped his arm about his sister's shoulders. "Well, there may have been a Band-Aid in it. At least you got Artie and me to agree on something." With a pat for Diana, a kiss for Lotti, who was absorbed in the paint cards she held fanned, and a mock salute for Arthur, Trace headed for the Whittingtons' private marina.

"Trace?"

Trace turned, but didn't stop. "Can't talk now, Dee. My true inner self wants to connect with the sea."

"About my idea," Diana persisted. "It's a little more than that."

Trace halted. He planted his feet wide apart, folded his arms and looked askance at his sister. "How little is a little more?"

"Now, Trace," Diana began, "don't get upset. The baroness might not even accept my invitation—"

"Oh, God!" Arthur grabbed the potted palm next to him as though for support.

Trace bore down on Diana, backing her to the edge of the pool. "The Baroness Oleska is coming here, to this house?"

"I don't know that she is for certain," Diana said, looking behind her, then back at Trace. "I only sent the invitation this morning."

Trace forced Diana to bend backward over the water. "I don't suppose there's a chance you neglected to put the correct postage on it?"

Eyes wide, Diana shook her head. "Brian took it to the post office on his way to the courthouse. I asked him to send it express mail." She swallowed. "Are you very angry with me, Trace?"

Trace pinned her with her own double image in the lenses of his glasses. "Just because you've compromised my lawsuit by inviting the woman I'm suing the pants off into the bosom of our little family?" Trace took a breath. "Nah."

Diana beamed.

Trace beamed back. "Not unless you consider this very angry!" Scooping Diana up in his arms, he held her out over the water.

"Oh, Trace, no! You wouldn't!" Diana's legs fluttered like hummingbird wings. "I just bought this outfit. It's pure silk!"

"Trace, put your sister down," Lotti commanded.

Gauging the expression in his mother's eyes, one he knew well, Trace played the dutiful son and set Diana on her feet, her back to the water.

"Thank you," Lotti said, nodding at Trace. She turned to her daughter, taking the hem of her jacket between her thumb and forefinger, and smiling. "My, that is a lovely silk." Then she raised her palms to the level of Diana's shoulders and pushed. Gazing down at the flailing woman sputtering water from her speechless lips, Lotti said, "Now it's moiré!"

Arthur Whittington V hooted with laughter at his sister's expense, and Lotti, shaking her head, returned to studying her paint samples. Neither of them noticed Trace slip into the house. Taking the steps of the cantilevered grand staircase by twos, he dashed into his room and headed straight for his bathroom. There, he wielded his razor at his fashionable smudge of beard. He'd be less easily recognized without it, saving himself the trouble of breaking some poor photographer's camera or his nose or both. He hadn't always reacted so violently to having his picture taken, he thought as he threw a few essentials into a sport bag. Only in the past five years, since he'd walked away from Whittington, Inc. He'd always rationalized that he was merely responding in kind to invasions of privacy, but lately he suspected he just couldn't bear to look at his own image, at what he'd become.

And could do nothing to change, he thought, as he sneaked down to the six-car garage. Tossing his bag into the Wrangler, he hopped in, and still shirtless and barefoot, sped away. The baroness, he had no doubt, would be unable to resist Diana's invitation to a "peace" summit. What better place to gather ammunition than in the enemy's camp? But when she arrived, he'd be noticeably absent. Her lawyers wouldn't be able to charge that his having so recently been her host was a tacit admission that his suit was frivolous.

Soon his fury at Diana subsided, and as he crossed the Southern Boulevard Bridge to the mainland, he savored the exhilaration of escape that always came with the wind in his hair. All he had to decide was where to go from here. Suddenly a smile broadened his clean-shaven face. He began picturing the secret paradise his childhood pal and current Hialeah buddy, the notoriously adulterous Cortland Rockwell III, had once described. Or maybe it was *pre-*

scribed, because the wet glistening bodies he was imagining were surely the antidote to the houseguest from hell. When that vampire with the press badge, the "Baroness Oleska," swooped down on Palm Beach, he'd be hundreds of miles away. Just he and as many pretty little things as one man could handle.

SHEATHING HER HANDS in the back pockets of her jeans, Sonny planted the treads of her hiking boots on the crest of Cara Mountain. It wasn't a majestic mountain or even a very tall mountain. But it was her father's little piece of paradise snuggled in a remote cranny of the Blue Ridge. She inhaled deeply of cool air scented with pine and gazed down at the indigo lake, teeming with bass and trout, and shimmering with a thousand mini-suns. Tucked into wooded niches around the lake were small cabins, clean, uncluttered and devoid of phones, radios, televisions—anything that dared to intrude on the peace of the mountain. Edward Chapin understood all too well the stresses his burned-out lodgers came to the mountain to flee. His daughter knew what had forced him from his electronics business and brought him to this retreat in the first place. No, not what. Who. Arthur Whittington V. And if it was the last thing she ever did, she'd make sure he paid for his reckless disregard. She'd—

"Ooooo! Whoa!" Sonny's hands flew from her pockets like birds frightened from their nests as her legs went into a split, instead of taking her back down the mountain as she had directed them to do. Casting an eye-popping glance at her feet, she saw the ground beneath them was slick with fat green dew-drenched needles. She felt like she was rolling pencils. More by accident than design, she latched onto a nearby branch of the treacherous shedding pine beside her. What she didn't realize was that it grew from the other part of the tree and had become tangled in adjacent branches. But by the time she found out, it was too late. Her weight had freed it to spring to its natural position, taking her with it. She was hanging over the side of the mountain.

She didn't look down. She didn't have to. She knew that about fifteen feet below was a dirt path, too narrow to break her fall. Her only choice was to backpedal and pray she could reclaim a foothold on the crest. The heels of her boots went at it like pickaxes, but all she managed to do was start a small avalanche of dirt clods, spiky needles and pointy broken branches.

Trace shook off pellets from the chunk of earth that had exploded above his head. "What the...?" He looked up. "Hey! Are you...?" He spat away the dirt that had lodged in the crease of his lips. "Are you crazy? You could kill somebody."

Over her dangling feet, Sonny gaped at the man looking up at her from the dangerous path below. Unlike most of her father's stressed-for-success refugees, he was clean-shaven, with a full head of well-groomed hair, and wearing generic sunglasses. He was different in another way. He wasn't exactly swift. "Really? Did it occur to you it could be me I kill unless you climb up here and help me?"

Removing his glasses, Trace squinted the woman into better focus. Even if a sleek plane of auburn hair wasn't spilling over her face, he wouldn't have been able to make out her features from where he stood. He could, however, testify that she had the cutest little behind he'd seen this side of the Atlantic, and he'd bet those cheeks weren't implants, either. Putting his glasses back on, he folded his arms across his chest. "Well, maybe I will climb up there and maybe, I won't. I am on vacation, you know," he said as earnestly as if he had a real job to vacation from. "I came up here to do some serious fishing, not rescue damsels in distress."

Sonny gasped as the branch dipped lower. "Look, buddy, you may get down to the lake faster than you imagined unless you do something quick, because if I go, I'm taking you with me."

Trace glanced to his right, down the gentle slope dotted with plenty of shrubbery to break a fall—eventually. Still, if she did take him out, it wouldn't be the kind of tumble he usually had in mind. "You may have a point," he said to her. "I'll be right there." He continued up the path.

"Stop!"

Halting, Trace looked up again. From this angle he got a better look at her legs, which were long and lean and probably devastating in bicycle shorts. "First, don't stop. Now, stop. What's a man to think?"

Imagining the branch was his neck, Sonny tightened her grip. "If you had a brain to think with, you'd have realized by now you're not on one of the designated hiking trails." She took a breath. "It isn't safe."

"Oh, I do apologize," Trace said, clutching his heart. "I'd be glad to go down and come up the right path if you'd like."

"No! You can't leave me now."

Trace cocked one eye and displayed a grin to match it. "You're not going to ask me to break the rules, are you?"

Sonny's arms were beginning to go numb. "Unless you get your miserable self up here in three seconds, I'll break more than the rules, if you catch my drift."

"You know, we're really going to have to talk about the mixed signals you send," Trace said, then moved farther along the path toward several protruding dead roots.

"Well, here's one I'm sure even you won't have trouble unscrambling."

Trace stopped and gazed up.

Sonny's legs danced like a marionette's as she tried to regrip the branch higher up. But she failed, exhausting most of her breath in the process. In spurts she informed him that the path ended just ahead of where he stood, on the other side of the roots. "You'll have to come straight up the side of the mountain."

"Oh." Trace suddenly realized that all the time he'd been taking advantage of the situation, unable to resist goading her, he'd really been gambling that the path would get him to her long before her strength or the branch gave way. Given his luck in Monte Carlo, he should have known better. His heart picking up pace, he searched for a foothold and something to grab on to, but all he came up with were handfuls of dirt. Crapped out again. He looked up and tried to keep his voice calm. "One unmixed signal deserves another, so I'll give it to you straight. You're going to have to let go of the branch."

"What?"

"It'll be all right. I'll catch you."

"And who's going to catch you?"

Trace decided against one last look behind him. Slipping his sunglasses into his hip pocket, he spread his legs, leaned his thighs into the mountain and reached up. "Trust me," he said. Then, swallowing hard, he added, "I'm lucky."

Sonny, too, took a hard swallow. "I can't do it."

"You can," Trace replied, trying to sound convincing.

"I won't."

"You have to."

"I—"

The mountainside erupted in a flurry of beating wings and shrill caws as Sonny, screaming and letting go of the snapped branch, plunged downward.

Straining his arms toward her, Trace shut his eyes against the dirt shower raining on him. When it stopped, he'd have bet that of the two of them, he was the more amazed that Sonny had slid into his arms. Clasping her thighs, he instinctively pinned her with his torso. After a moment he was pleasantly surprised to discover that not only were they both safe, but his cheek was pressed against the cleavage of two mounds so naturally soft and round he nostalgically recognized them as the real thing. Ferreting out the grit between his teeth with the tip of his tongue, he grinned up at her. "Guess I caught your drift, after all. Are you…"

Seeing her face up close, he paused. She wasn't gorgeous or beautiful or even attractive in the way that women talented in makeup artistry were. She was just clean-skinned and silver-eyed and auburn-haired—no roots. She was something he hadn't seen in so long he couldn't help staring. *Pretty*. Scared as she was, she was just plain pretty.

"Are you all right?" Trace asked.

As fast as her heart was still racing, Sonny knew it would never catch up with her stomach, which had gone on down the mountain without her. "I will be," she said, trying to make something of the man's face, blackened with rich mountain soil. But all she could see was a pair of smoky eyes rimmed with thick lashes that made the dirt surrounding them look faded. Eyes she was certain went with an equally arresting nose and mouth. It was time she resisted arrest. "As soon as my feet touch solid ground."

She tried to wriggle lower in his embrace, but Trace held her steady. The truth was, her soap-and-water scent was intoxicating senses he had thought were permanently jaded by twelve-hundred-dollar-an-ounce perfume. He couldn't bear to put her down. Not yet. "But this path isn't safe," he said. "You told me so yourself."

Maybe he wasn't so different from the men who came to her father's mountain, after all, Sonny thought. Men who figured that as long as they were going back to nature, why not take the mountain man's daughter with them? What could be more natural? Sometimes she got a kick out of playing along, doing her Daisy Mae imitation and chewing on a reed until it became necessary to use the defenses she'd learned growing up in Chicago and living in New York. Still, she didn't see a need to go quite that far yet. "I know the path well, so it's safe enough for me," she said. "And of course for things that crawl on their bellies."

Trace gazed up at Sonny, as if in thought.

Sonny looked down at Trace. She'd have to find another way to handle this one. He didn't seem to comprehend that he'd just been insulted.

"Okay, guy, you've had your fun. Now put me down."

She pressed her palms into a pair of shoulders thick and strong as the padded arms of her favorite reading chair.

To no avail. Then the man inhaled sharply.

"Okay," he said, and let go of her.

Gasping, she slid down his body.

Trace didn't catch her again until her lips reached the point at which he wanted them. Opposite his.

Sonny stretched her toes as far beneath her as she could, but she still couldn't touch the ground. Not that it mattered. With his lips so close to hers, she'd suddenly lost all feeling in her toes. "You think you're pretty slick, don't you?"

Feeling her breath waft across his mouth like a gentle sea breeze, Trace didn't feel the least bit slick or sophisticated. "No," he whispered back. "I just think you're pretty." His gaze roamed her uncomplicated features. "And kind of sweet."

"Uh-huh." Sonny didn't have to ask if he'd been getting results with a line like that. Noting her fascination with the curve of his lower lip and the way her fingers were drawn to the nape of his neck, she knew he didn't need any line. Still, he did need taking down a notch. "And I thought I knew every variety of snake on this mountain."

Although the woman had just called him a reptile, her touch was so light and refreshingly unpremeditated, Trace found himself meditating on what her lips might taste like. Slowly he began lowering her to the path... "This may surprise you, but I wouldn't blame you if you called me worse. I shouldn't have teased you the way I did. Sometimes I get carried away."

"Really?" she whispered, inhaling his masculine scent.

With his lips, Trace limned her mouth. "Hmm. Just ask my sister."

Sonny's mouth began a circumnavigation of its own, finding the mix of brisk aftershave and earth scents a surprisingly heady brew. "What I meant is," she murmured, "are you really sorry?"

"Mortified," Trace murmured back, exaggerating only

slightly. If he'd toyed with her predicament a second longer, she might have been hurt. "Why?"

Sonny looked directly into his eyes. She started to speak, hesitated, then without questioning how she knew, decided that she had earlier been wrong about him. "I thought so. Men of conscience are so rare these days."

Trace winced. If she knew who he was and how, for a price, he'd left a giant corporation and the fates of thousands of people in the hands of his idiot brother, she couldn't have said that about him. And the damnedest thing was, what she thought of him mattered. In response to the alarming notion that what a woman thought of him actually mattered, he attempted to fend her off with his most devilish grin. "Not men of bad conscience."

Sonny buried a soft laugh in the crook of his warm neck. Instantly she thought of her father and wondered why. Nothing about this man in any way resembled Edward Chapin, unless it was the scent of his skin. No. Though Sonny found it clean and appealingly male, she knew it was as distinct from her father's as the smell of the pines on Cara Mountain was from that of the cedars. What was it, then, that reminded her of the man she admired most in the world?

With her cheek pressed to his and her hands clasped about his neck, Trace began to feel something he tried hard never to feel about a woman, something more than protective. Responsible. Even if he hadn't found her dangling from a tree limb over the edge of a cliff, he still would have felt called to look after her, as though any harm that came to her would be his fault. Funny, that was exactly the way he'd come to feel about Whittington, Inc., that he was to blame for its foundering because he had refused to fight for its helm, to risk another humiliating defeat. Actually, not so funny. And as for the delectable woman in his arms, rather than looking after her, he ought to be watching out for her and the trap she was laying, however unknowingly. He had to get them both down from this height to where the atmosphere was less rare and he was less apt to suffer delusions.

As her rescuer at last set her down on her feet, atop his own because the path was too narrow to accommodate them both, Sonny knew what it was about him that called her father to mind. It wasn't the way he looked or sounded or smelled, but how he made her feel. Trusting. Standing on his insteps, sharing with him a precarious foothold on the side of a mountain, she nevertheless felt safe. Lifting her head, she gazed into his eyes, the promising color of pre-dawn over the Blue Ridge. "I don't believe you have a bad conscience about anything."

Trace was now certain the elevation was affecting his judgment, because not only had the adorable freckle on the bridge of her nose banished all thoughts of fleeing to the safety of his cabin, he wanted what she had said to be true. *Mon dieu,* he had to put a stop to this. There was no telling where the stirrings of desire for an upright conscience might lead, certainly not to any good. Closing his eyes, he rested his lips on hers, his breath catching on their plumpness, his mind's eye conjuring all things round, soft and delicious. "You wouldn't say that if you knew what I was thinking right now."

The left side of Sonny's brain informed her she was insane. The right side wondered how it would feel to part her lips beneath his, to fan the sparks he was igniting into an all-consuming fire. Giving thanks she was right-brained, she blew soft slow syllables across his lips. "Tell me what you're thinking."

Trace wondered how he could have played with fire all these years and never before melted, as he was doing now. Trailing his lips across her cheek, he said, "Of how sweet you taste. I was thinking of how unbearably hot and sweet you taste." With his mouth, he outlined the delicate shell of her ear. "Like some rare and exotic spice."

Sonny had been told she was rare before, usually by first dates who couldn't understand her objection to sleeping with them, even after they'd so generously offered to spring for the condoms—she should pardon the expression. But no man had ever claimed she was rare *and* exotic. Suddenly she saw herself as a gorgeously plumed and graceful bird, and—heaven help her—she wanted to fly. Tilting her head back, she offered him her neck. "What else?"

Trace paused, ran his thumb down the satin column, then dropped kisses on it. So, this was what it was like to kiss springtime, he thought, to touch your lips to a gentle breeze, to inhale the fragrance of the sun in a meadow of wild-flowers. Yet, it was all too sweet, too simple, too innocent a sensation to be happening to him. "What else was I thinking?" he asked, echoing her question as he brushed his lips toward her mouth. "Of how corny our meeting was. Confess. You set the whole thing up, didn't you."

Not in her wildest, most erotic dreams could she have imagined such a meeting, Sonny thought. "All I'll confess is that I wish I had," she whispered back, faintly impressing a small bite on his lower lip. "But the truth is, I was just hanging out." As he delivered soft laughter with tantalizing nibbles of his own, she realized she wanted him to do more, much more. She wanted him to do things that would make dangling over the side of a mountain seem as safe as an afternoon nap on her sofa. With her visions came an encouraging groan. "What else?"

To her question came no answer.

"Come on," she murmured, nudging one corner of his mouth. "What else is on your mind?"

Still no answer, and his incredible kisses had stopped.

Sonny opened her eyes on the most beautiful man she'd ever seen, suddenly afraid she'd never really know him. "Tell me, please."

The man's gaze shifted right, then left, then narrowed on Sonny. "Maybe you'd better tell me."

A crease formed between Sonny's brows. "Tell you what?"

"How far it is to the bottom of this mountain."

Before she could reply, the path crumbled beneath Trace's feet.

3

"WHO IS HE, DAD?" Sitting beside an unconscious Trace on her father's bed, Sonny pressed a plastic bag filled with cracked ice to the swelling near his left temple, where it had struck a tree stump.

Edward Chapin stood over his daughter, plucking twigs and dirt clumps from the tangles of her hair. "I would have thought you two had time for introductions, considering how far you tumbled down Cara Mountain together."

Sonny relinquished a smile. "Well, he did shout out some rather colorful names, but I don't think any of them were his."

"Not unless one of them was Terry Wright," Chapin replied. "We had quite a long talk when he checked in last night. Seems like a bright young man. He told me he drove up here for the trout and some peace and quiet." Reaching around Sonny, he lifted Trace's right eyelid to reveal a dilated pupil ringed in blue. "I'm not sure he'll get much fishing in, but he certainly won't be able to complain about a lack of rest."

Sonny begrudged her father a smile. "I don't think a concussion is quite what he had in mind."

"No, I don't suppose so." Chapin craned a look at his daughter. "But why would he have? He didn't know *you'd* be here."

"Dad?"

"Yes, love?"

She slapped the cold wet bag into the palm of his hand. "Get some fresh ice."

Chapin made a face as he pinched one corner of the bag between his thumb and forefinger, then wiped his palm on his flannel shirt. "Feels just like a trout. You'll forgive the pun, but I'll never understand the lure of fishing."

Sonny pointed him toward the kitchen in the cabin that served as both his home and the retreat's office. After he'd gone, she took a cloth from the basin of warm water on the nightstand. Wringing it out, she gently wiped the dirt from Trace's forehead, then from his lowered lids, feathered with thick, black lashes. As she removed the dark outlines on either side of his nose, she noticed how straight it was, and strong. It posed an intriguing contrast to his sensual lips, which parted at the touch of her cloth-covered fingertip. When she came to the narrow cleft of his chin, she removed the cloth, placing her bare finger to his skin. The conflicting textures of stubble and tiny mounds of flesh forced a sudden and deep catch in her breathing.

"Not bad-looking when you get him cleaned up, is he?"

Sonny started, then took the bag of ice Chapin handed to her and applied it to Trace's head. Ignoring the implication in her father's question, as well as the twinkle in his eye, she said, "His face isn't done yet."

Chapin peered over her shoulder. "Two eyes, a nose, a mouth. Looks done to me."

Sonny smiled crookedly. "What I meant was that he won't be at his most attractive for at least another ten years. That's when a man's true character starts to show." *When time—and life—have softened the lines, etched away the starkness, stamped him with the mark of a man who's won and lost, but never shrunk from the battle.* And strangely she had the feeling this man's toughest battle lay ahead of him.

"That's what your mother used to say," Chapin replied. "Every time I'd notice a new crag in my face, she'd tell me it was a badge of honor for having slain another dragon." Sighing, he crossed to the nightstand and picked up the copy of *Celebrity* lying open at the Baroness Oleska's article on the Whittingtons. "You know, Sonny, sometimes I comfort myself that your mother never knew there was one dragon I couldn't slay."

Flint struck steel in the look Sonny blazed at her father. "Don't say that, Dad! Mom would have been as proud of you as I am, and just as angry that you were used." She poked her finger at her story. "Besides, that fight isn't over yet."

Tugging his lower lip as he focused on the article, Chapin walked to the foot of the bed. "I meant to talk to you about that, Sonny. These pieces you've been writing on the Whittingtons…" He dropped the magazine next to Trace's legs. "I think you're making a mistake."

Releasing the cloth she was freshening in the basin, Sonny turned to her father. "How can you say that after what they've done to you, to Chapin Industries?"

"I know how you feel, Sonny." He rubbed the back of his neck. "Don't you think there were nights I stayed awake thinking of nothing but how to get back at young Arthur Whittington? But revenge isn't the answer."

"It's the only answer I've got, Dad," she said, towel-scrubbing her hands as though she were wiping out all traces of the Whittingtons.

Chapin hastened to his daughter's side, and taking her hands in his, brought her to her feet. "Sonora, I want you to ask yourself if personal attacks on the Whittingtons will bring back Chapin Industries. Will they bring back all those lost jobs? Of course not. All they'll do is turn you, as they would have turned me, into a lonely and bitter human being. If I can move on with my life, honey, why can't you?"

Withdrawing her hands, Sonny turned and gazed down at Terry Wright. He was so serene in his unconsciousness she almost envied him. But serenity was a luxury she couldn't afford until she had exacted retribution from the Whittingtons. Her father was certainly free to make his peace in his own way, but so was she.

"I'm sorry, Dad. I can't stand by and let Arthur Whittington get away with corporate murder while his brother, Trace, acts as his accomplice by refusing to lift a finger to stop him.''

''Of course you can't. I didn't raise you to be a by-stander.''

She paused, her gray eyes clouding. ''If you're trying to confuse me, you're doing a first-rate job.''

Chapin laid gentle but firm hands on Sonny's shoulders. ''Look, I'll grant you that the Baroness Oleska probably isn't making it any easier for Arthur Whittington to put his family's financial house in order. Maybe she can even be instrumental in his downfall. But what will you, Sonny Chapin, have accomplished?'' Stepping closer, he looked long and hard into the eyes of his only child. ''If you're going be an instrument of change, Sonny, make sure the change isn't a destructive one.''

Her forehead furling, Sonny looked once more at the man whose form filled the length of her father's bed. A man of conscience, she had called him before they came crashing down the mountain together. And he had said she was sweet. Would he still say that if he learned she was a pseudonymous reporter for a high-class tabloid who was on the lam from a process server? As she retrieved the afghan her mother had crocheted from the chair on the other side of the bed, she decided it didn't matter what he would think of her. She couldn't let any man's opinion, not even her dear father's, keep her from finishing the demolition job she had begun a year ago with that first wrecking ball of a column she had hurled at the Whittingtons.

Still, as she laid the afghan over Terry Wright, noting the workingman's build, and the clean honest lines of his face, she knew she did care what he thought of her. The fall off the mountain wasn't the only one she'd taken that morning, or even the most dangerous.

On the other hand, she thought, brightening, why should he find out she was the Baroness Oleska? Other than Jack and a few staffers at the magazine, only her father knew about her alter ego. And she had pledged Dad to secrecy long ago. Not that she'd had to. He hadn't been exactly thrilled when she'd left her last job as a crime reporter in a small Midwestern city, where a major crime was violating lawn-watering restrictions. Nor had he been totally sympathetic to her lament that reporting dull hard news—in contrast to juicy gossip—invariably translated into low pay. Still, she'd been able to mollify him with assurances that she intended for *Celebrity* to be nothing more than a stepping stone to *Time* or *Newsweek*. She just hadn't been able to make good on her assurances.

Soon, though, she promised herself. Just as soon as she'd finished with the Whittingtons. She'd get her career back on track, become the journalist she'd always dreamed of being. Then she wouldn't have to hide what she did for a living from anyone, especially not from the man in whose strong secure arms she had avalanched down a mountainside.

"Dad?" Sonny's gaze suddenly narrowed on the deep rise and fall of Trace's chest. "Don't you think he should have come to by now?"

Edward Chapin took another look at Trace's pupils. "It's two hours to the nearest doctor. I'm sure that by the time we get him there, he'll come around. But you're probably right," he said, straightening. "We shouldn't take chances. I'll bring Henry and Luke from the lake to get him into the truck."

After her father left, Sonny sat beside Trace. She was about to reapply the ice bag that had slipped onto the pillow, when she saw a flicker of movement beneath his lids. "Hello-o-o," she whispered. "Anybody home?"

Getting no response, she gently bounced on the bed a few times in an attempt to jump-start him. But he remained as immobile as the tree stump that had halted their descent down the mountain.

"Mr. Wright? Terry?" Pulling back the afghan, she lifted his hand, then let it go. It fell like a brick, missing the bed and dangling above the floor. Sonny laid it on his chest, then deciding she'd created a ghastly pose, straightened his arm at his side. She sighed, glanced around the ceiling, whistled a few bars of "She'll Be Comin' Round the Mountain," then sidled a peek at Trace. A smile broke the pucker of her lips as she saw a muscle in his jaw flinch. Jumping off the bed, she ran to the foot, unlaced his boots and pulled them off. Cupping her hand beneath his left heel, she lifted his leg in the air.

"Darned if you don't weigh a ton when you're knocked out," she murmured, renewing her respect for Henry and Luke. Starting at the ball of his stockinged foot, she ran the tip of her finger up and down the sole. After making several trips without eliciting a response, she yanked off the sock and went at his arch with all five fingers. Nothing.

Sonny panicked. "Oh, God, please don't let him be paralyzed for life." She let go of Trace's foot, which dropped like a bomb, and brought praying hands to her lips. "What am I thinking? Even if he's not paralyzed, he'll sue. He'll sue Dad for millions and take Cara Mountain away from him." Scrunching a fistful of hair at the top of her head, she turned her back on Trace. Of course, he could belong to that religion that doesn't believe in lawyers, she thought, grasping at hope. No, it was doctors they don't believe in. "Damn."

Whipping back around, she dashed to the head of the empty side of the bed and, climbing on, knelt over Trace. "Look, Mr. Wright. The accident was my fault. If you have to sue somebody, sue me." She brought her lips close to his, then spoke slowly and hypnotically, trying to reach his unconscious mind. "Sue...me-e-e."

Trace's eyes popped open. "I'm considering it."

Sonny screamed and backed clear to the wall, knocking over the floor lamp next to the lounge chair. After several attempts and much clatter, she succeeded in righting it. She gaped at Trace, her hand flattened over her pounding heart. "My God! You scared me half to death."

Easing himself to a sitting position, Trace touched his fingertips to the protrusion on his head and winced. "Come on back here and I'll be glad to see what I can do about the other half." Then, recalling how they had met and her altercation with the lamp not a moment ago, he added, "On second thought, stay right where you are."

Still panting with fright, Sonny nevertheless felt her hackles rise. "I can certainly understand your being upset, Mr. Wright, even none too happy to see me. But after all, you did take that path despite clearly marked warnings to stay off it."

"Which would make me either illiterate or suicidal." Trace rubbed his aching eyes. "Believe me, there were no such warnings."

Sonny's breathing halted entirely. The arrogance of the man. "If you would care to come out to the mountain with me, I can prove to you—"

"That you're a menace to public safety?" Trace looked down at the shredded sleeve of his shirt, then up at Sonny. "No, thanks. Been there, done that."

"Mr. Wright," Sonny began, squelching the urge to raise a lump on the other side of his hard head. "You're just going to have to accept that you and you alone are responsible for having been on that path."

"Why is the whole world suddenly so concerned about my sense of responsibility?" Lying back on the pillow, Trace bent his arm across his eyes. "And why do you keep calling me Mr. Right? I feel like a door prize at a ladies' luncheon."

Stepping close, Sonny leaned over Trace, her gaze a question mark. "Because that's your name. Don't you remember?"

I do now, Trace thought. When he'd checked in, he'd used an alias despite the assurances of his friend, Cort Rockwell, that neither of their infamous names were known in this remote little haven. "Of course I remember. But now that we're forever bonded like people in a story on

Rescue 911, I thought you might call me Terry." Lifting his arm, he looked up at her out of the corner of his eye. "And what may I have the pleasure of calling you, other than the obvious names that spring so readily to mind?"

"Sonny Chapin."

The proprietor's young wife? Trace felt a stab of disappointment, but told himself it was probably a broken rib. Anyway, on second look, she wasn't as adorable as he'd first thought when he held her in his arms on that damned mountain.

"I can think of a few names for you, too, you know," Sonny added, folding her arms across her chest and thinking the only perfect man was an unconscious one.

"I can just imagine," Trace replied. "But there's no need for formalities. Just plain Galahad will do."

"Gala—?" Although the bait was tempting, Sonny wasn't biting. "Sorry, we're fresh out of purple hearts today."

Trace propped himself on his elbows. "Look, maybe I didn't exactly take a bullet for you, but I did mow down a few prickly bushes before they had a chance to scrub that cute little freckle off your nose."

Self-consciously, Sonny covered one side of her nose. Jack had hated her few freckles. He had even suggested she bleach them. Suddenly she felt as though she were plunging down the mountain all over again, and it was thrilling. "All right. I thank you," she said. "My father thanks you, my freckle thanks you."

"Your father?"

"Edward Chapin. He owns Cara Mountain, which he named for my mother. This is his room."

Trace looked around. "The man I talked to last night is your father?" When she nodded, he realized she suddenly appeared even more adorable than he had first thought.

"And speaking of Dad," Sonny said, "I'd better find him before he drags Henry and Luke back from the lake." She started for the door. "They won't be pleased when they discover that after they let the big one get away on your account, you aren't dying, after all.''

Trace made a discovery of his own. He found he didn't want her to leave, not even for a moment. "Sorry I can't oblige Henry and Luke. By the way, who are they?"

"Dad's fishing and hunting guides," Sonny replied, coming to a stop. "They carried you here."

Trace frowned. He didn't relish the vision he'd just had of himself being carted off, an unheroic lump, in this woman's sight. "They must be real big guides," he said petulantly in an attempt to regain his dignity.

Picturing Henry and Luke, Sonny hid a chuckle behind her hand. "They are. Now, if you'll excuse me..." As she reached the door, she heard an agonized moan. She rushed back to Trace. "Are you all right? What's the matter?"

Trace made a mental scramble for a complaint to justify the groan he had calculated would keep her with him. "It's my legs," he said, lying back. "I'm not sure I have feeling in them."

Sonny felt sickened. Then, she remembered she had seen the afghan undulate over his thighs when he'd first sat up, as though he were repositioning his legs. Sauntering to the foot of the bed, she stared at his feet—one bare and one stockinged—protruding from the afghan. She reached for the bare one.

"Don't you touch me, woman!" Drawing his legs up from beneath the blanket, Trace plastered himself against the headboard. "Ms. Chapin, I think you must have a foot fetish."

Sonny's jaw dropped as her eyes grew wide. "You felt me tickling you!"

Trace tucked his hands into his armpits. "A corpse could have felt that. Who taught you how to tickle—interrogators for the Chinese Army?"

"And who taught you how to act—an undertaker?"

Trace smiled. "Aren't you at least relieved to know I'll walk again?"

Actually she was. But she'd no sooner acknowledged it than a fresh wave of panic engulfed her. Just how long before he had felt her tickle his foot had he been conscious? Instinctively her gaze darted to the magazine lying beside him.

Trace's gaze followed hers and instantly recognized the cover of the current issue of *Celebrity*. Now he not only wanted the Baroness Oleska's head, he wanted Cortland Rockwell III's for swearing that no one at Cara Mountain knew a Whittington from a whetstone. Thank God he'd known better than to trust the lovable but completely unreliable Cort and had concocted an alias.

Sonny and Trace raised their eyes to each other.

"My father reads a lot," she said, leaning across him, scooping up the magazine and moving to the nightstand. She opened the top drawer.

"Your father?" Trace lowered his feet to the floor. "I have a hard time believing a solid guy like him would waste his time on a rag like that."

Placing the magazine in the drawer, Sonny slammed it shut, harder than she'd intended. "What exactly do you mean, 'rag'?"

Trace laughed, as though surprised she had to ask. "What I mean exactly is that your father strikes me as an intelligent human being who would know the difference between the truth and a pack of pernicious lies when he saw it."

Sonny entwined her arms tightly. "Proof that *Celebrity* doesn't print lies."

"I respect your father," Trace said, rising, too quickly. Circles of light burst before his eyes. But refusing to sit back down, he waited for Sonny's face to come back into view. "And I respect how you feel about him. But have you read that piece of garbage?"

Garbage? Sonny propped her hands on her waist. "Yes! Have you?"

"Not willingly and not entirely." True enough. He'd

only read what the baroness had written about the Whittingtons.

Sonny issued a derisive laugh. "Yet you're certain it trades in untruths."

"Come on, Sonny." Trace circled behind her. "You may be a klutz, but I can tell you're too smart to believe everything you read."

Rounding, Sonny sent him a scorching gaze. "At least I'm not so cynical I don't believe *anything* I read. And I am not a klutz!" Promptly she took a step forward—onto his bare toes.

Trace squeezed his eyes shut and bit his tongue.

Wincing as though she were the injured party, Sonny slowly removed her boot from his instep. "I am so sorry."

"Fine." Trace looked down at her. "Just don't dare tell me you feel my pain. No court would hold me responsible for what I would do to you."

Sonny heaved a sigh of self-disgust. "It happens whenever I get really passionate."

Trace's eyes filled with both terror and intrigue at the possibilities.

"Not that kind of passionate," she said.

She looked so unhappy with herself Trace couldn't help softening. In fact, he wanted to take her in his arms and kiss away *her* hurt. "There are worse things than feeling passionate," he said. Like not feeling at all. Suddenly it occurred to him that since he'd met her that morning, he'd felt more emotion than he'd felt in the past year, even if it was mostly in reaction to pain. Any woman who could make him feel again was a woman he had to know better. But first he had to find out what, if anything, she knew about him. He had to know if she'd read that article in *Celebrity*.

"So tell me," he said, walking to the foot of the bed to retrieve his hiking boots and socks. "What have you read in *Celebrity* lately that warrants such a passionate defense of its journalistic integrity?"

Sonny had only moments ago sworn she wouldn't care what he thought if he knew she was the Baroness Oleska. But as she watched the rippling expanse of his strong straight back, the power in his shoulders as he pulled on his boots, she had to find out if he'd read her feature. "I've found those articles by Baroness Oleska on the Whittingtons to be...interesting."

Lacing his boots, Trace froze. Slowly he sat up and clamped a strong grip on his thighs. He had to get a grip on something. "You have to be kidding." Rising, he turned to Sonny. "The baro— That parasite?"

Her heart plummeted. The only good news was that she no longer had to wonder what he thought of the baroness. "Why do you call her a parasite?"

"Parasite, leech—take your pick." Shoving his hands into his pockets, Trace walked toward her. "Anybody who feeds off the private lives of others is a bloodsucker. It's too bad, too. Whoever Oleska is, she's a damn good writer. She should be able to make a lot better use of her talent." And he certainly wished she would.

Things were improving, Sonny thought glumly. At least she was a talented bloodsucker. "But the Whittingtons aren't ordinary private citizens like you and me. From what I've read in the baroness's columns, they hold a majority stake in a huge conglomerate. They have a responsibility—"

"So does the baroness. To the truth."

The truth about Madame X leapt to Sonny's tongue. How she longed to tell him the baroness got her information from a reliable source. "But even if you only believed half of what she writes, you'd have to conclude that the Whittingtons are silly, frivolous people. People with too much money and too few brains to know how to handle it." She sank onto the mattress. "Except, apparently, for Trace Whittington."

Trace cocked his head to one side. "Why do you say that?"

Sonny gazed up into eyes so intense and direct she knew Terry Wright was no Trace Whittington. He'd never run away, even from defeat, as Trace had. "I read that he was the son who really cared about Whittington Enterprises, Inc. When he was a kid, he worked in the factories of the various Whittington companies. Later he graduated from MIT with honors, then went to the Wharton School of Business, where he displayed the promise of genius at corporate restructuring." Jumping up, she waved her finger before Trace. "He's the one who ought to be running Whittington!"

Trace gulped. She made him feel things all right. First pain, now guilt. "I thought I read he tried to take over the company and lost."

"And then what did he do? Did he take it like a man and try again?"

"Didn't he?"

Sonny exhaled. "No. He ran away and took comfort with half of the socialites on two continents."

"Which of their halves?" Seeing she hadn't appreciated his humor, Trace cleared his throat. "You know how the press overplays those things." It had certainly grossly exaggerated his reputation as a ladies' man, and in any case, he wasn't proud of it.

"Regardless, he's still a coward."

Trace recoiled, then looked away. For a man whose emotions had only recently come back from the grave, they were doing a remarkable job of tearing his insides out. He didn't think he could look her in the eye, but when he felt her soft gaze on him, he met it.

"You know, it's funny," she said. "I hardly know you, yet I sense you'd never run from a fight, especially if you believed in what you were fighting for."

Trace stood transfixed by the luminosity—the faith—in her silvery eyes. Suddenly he wanted nothing more than to justify that faith. He wanted to be the man she believed him to be. He almost believed he could. But how, when the man he really was was a man she despised? Deflated, he sat down beside her. "Obviously you have nothing but contempt for this Trace Whittington."

Sonny laughed to herself and at her rotten luck. She'd finally met a man she instinctively knew she could respect, only to discover he thought she was a leech. All right, a gifted leech. "No more than you have for the Baroness Oleska," she said.

Which is only a little less than I have for myself right now, Trace thought. What was it about this woman that compelled him to look in the mirror, really look at himself for the first time in years? If she'd been Gabrielle—any one of the Gabrielles he'd known—her disparaging assessment of him would have been like so much lint on his tuxedo, something to be brushed off and forgotten. But from the moment she'd looked at him with those huge gray eyes of hers—as though she could see through to his soul—and told him he was a man of conscience, he'd fallen under her spell. For the first time in his life a woman believed he had intrinsic worth. Okay, so she thought he was some guy named Terry Wright. He still couldn't dismiss that while she'd called Trace Whittington a coward, she'd also said he was the son who ought to be running Whittington, Inc. Not only did her faith in him make her sexier than a whole harem of Gabrielles, it made him think seriously about signing his trust over to Arthur for just the chance to prove she was right about him.

It was definitely checkout time. "I guess we're even, then," he said.

"I guess," Sonny replied, feeling not the least bit even with him. He was obviously a successful man, like most of those who stayed at her father's mountain retreat. And she was...a bloodsucker?

Frowning, she rose and crossed to the window. *Maybe I am a leech,* she thought, *but that only makes Arthur Whittington a piranha, ripping the flesh from healthy corporations and leaving nothing but the skeletons.* That was all he'd left of Chapin Industries after he'd acquired it, then ousted her father and his trusted management. No, she decided, gazing at Cara Mountain. As long as Arthur Whittington was swimming on Wall Street, she'd stick to him until he was drained drier than the bones of Chapin Industries. And if she could close the world's playgrounds to Trace Whittington at the same time, so much the better.

Then why didn't that prospect fill her with as much satisfaction as it once had? Only this morning, in fact, before she'd fallen into Terry Wright's arms.

Watching her at the window, Trace tried not to think about how different she was from other women, how basic and forthright, or about how she believed in him. He tried to ignore visions of the two of them lying on the rug in front of the fire in his cabin, visions of learning about her and learning from her. To do that, he'd have to play the impostor, Terry Wright. Sure, he could do it. After all, he'd been impersonating Trace Whittington for years. But as he finished lacing up his boots, he knew his days of putting over cons on the opposite sex—and on himself—had ended on Cara Mountain that morning when he'd caught Sonny in his arms. She was the one woman who deserved the whole truth and nothing but.

"Sonny?"

She turned toward him.

He took a step in her direction, then stopped. "Look, I'm fine now and there's no harm done." *Yet.* "I think it's best I be on my way."

Knowing she ought to be glad to see him go and take his opinions of the baroness with him, she also knew she wanted him to stay. She wanted to know everything about him, where he came from, what he did. What his dreams and hopes were. She stood before him. "But you just arrived last night. What about all the fish you had your heart set on catching? Henry and Luke are the best guides in this part of the state."

"I'm sure they are, but—"

"I won't come near you if that's what you're worried about," she said, backing away and raising her palms. "I promise."

Trace closed the gap she had opened and gazed down into her eyes. He never wanted to forget the light in those eyes, the trust. Skimming the curve of her cheek with the backs of his fingers, he said, "You don't understand, Sonny Chapin. If I stay, I'm going to want you near. Very near."

Sonny's lids flickered as her pulse quickened to his touch. "Is that bad?"

"Uh-huh. It will make our freefall down the mountain seem like a trip down a playground slide." He had to force himself to tear his hand from the feel of her skin. "Trust me. I know what I'm doing."

She'd tell him about the baroness, Sonny reasoned, in time. In time she'd make him understand why she'd had to do whatever she could to bring down the Whittingtons, to stop them from destroying other businesses like Chapin Industries. "So do I, Terry. And I'm not afraid to—"

"Be afraid. I'm not the man you think I am. I'd only disappoint you."

Sonny swallowed. "Nobody's really who anyone else thinks they are. Besides, I'm over twenty-one and you've given me fair warning."

"Be especially afraid of a man who gives you fair warning, Sonny. It's one of the oldest tricks in the book."

As he looked away, Sonny sensed he was trying to convince himself as much as he was her. Drawing his gaze back to hers, she said, "Maybe so. But can you look into my eyes and honestly tell me you're out to use me?"

Feeling her magic charming the truth from him, Trace nevertheless knew he had to keep it hidden. He didn't want her hoping for something he couldn't give her. "Using women is one of the things I do best. But I'm not a total cad. The arrangement has always been mutual."

Sonny wagged her head as she made a tsking sound. "Such a sad story." When he didn't return her gentle tease, she raked a strand of dark hair back from his forehead. "Has it really been that bad, Terry?"

"It's been that bad," Trace said, catching her hand and holding it, running his thumb over her soft palm. "And it's been mostly my fault. That's why I don't want things between us to go any farther. I don't deserve better than what I've had for too long now, and you're definitely better."

Better? Sonny closed her eyes, trying to shut out the knowledge of her duplicity. But eliminating her sight only made the feel of his hand clasping hers warmer and her guilt stronger. Yet she couldn't dislodge the growing conviction that their meeting, though truly accidental, had been no coincidence. The attraction between them was obviously too strong, too needy.

Opening her eyes, she squeezed her fingers around his hand. "Then if that's the way you feel, fight for me!"

Trace released her and stepped back. "Would you mind repeating that?"

Sonny came near, running her hands over the hard planes of his chest, curving them around his shoulders. "I think two people should be willing to fight for and beside each other. Whatever your battles are, I'm willing to…"

Grabbing her head, Trace began rooting through her hair.

"What are you doing?"

"Looking for a fracture. Obviously I'm not the only one who got hit on the head falling down that mountain."

"Stop!" Pushing his hands away, Sonny swept her hair from her eyes. "I know you're thinking we're practically strangers. But my parents knew they'd met the right person the moment they first laid eyes on each other. And they were together thirty-two years."

Trace sat on the bed and rested his head in his hands.

"What's wrong, Terry?"

"I may not be as well as I thought I was." He looked up at her. "You're actually making sense to me." *Sense?* Did it make sense that in the course of a single day, much of which he'd spent unconscious, this little witch could make him believe he could win control of Whittington, win her? Strangely, according to the weird logic he'd been operating under ever since he came to this place, yes. "Sonny, I swear this is the damnedest thing that's ever happened to me."

"Me, too," she said, kneeling before him. "Why don't we be damned together?"

His answer was to take her face in his hands and plunder her sweet mouth. As he lifted her onto his lap and wrapped her in his arms, he held back a tear. Then, grateful he could feel so much simple joy, grateful to the woman in his arms, he let it go.

Sonny caught the droplet on her lips, then touched her tongue to the salty taste of it. She sensed there was a whole deep well of feeling inside this man just waiting to be tapped by the right woman. And his kiss had told her he believed she was the right woman. Still, as she clasped her hands around his neck, she saw bewilderment in his expression. "Scared?" she asked softly.

Turning her in his arms, Trace pinned her beneath him. He splayed his fingers across her cheek, rubbed his thumb over her lips, then claimed them.

"I guess not," she whispered, snuggling into his embrace and hooking her leg over his.

Trace ran his palm up her calf, over the back of her thigh. He moved to kiss her once more, then stopped. What had he been thinking? If he tried again to wrestle Whittington away from Arthur and lost, which was as good as a bet got, he'd forfeit his trust fund. But worse, if he failed to get control of the company, he'd forfeit Sonny's faith in him. Maybe things *were* happening too fast. He needed time to think, to plan. He had so much to accomplish before he could risk Sonny's finding out who he really was.

He lifted her leg from his and stood. "Look, Sonny. One of us has to keep a clear head about this. I'm not ready..."

"No one's ever ready to fall in love." She came to his side. "Don't go, Terry."

"But you don't understand. There are things I have to—"

The door banged against the wall. "What you doin' outta bed, boy?"

Trace saw two six-foot-two-inch two-hundred pounders lumber toward him. They were identical, and judging from their long red braids and redder lips, they could have been women. He glimpsed the bulges in the bibs of their denim overalls. No doubt about it, they were women.

Amused at his stunned amazement, Sonny looped her arm through his. "Mr. Wright, I'd like you to meet Henrietta and Lucinda Barrow, Dad's right- and left-hand women."

Trace stood speechless as each of the twins how do'd him with a bone-crushing handshake.

"What you starin' at, boy?" Luke asked. "Hain't you never seen twins afore?"

Trace knew his mouth was still hanging open but couldn't seem to shut it to make a reply.

"Still tetched," Henry said, looking at her sister and pointing to her own head. "We'd better get him to the doc's, like Mr. Chapin said."

As they flanked him, Trace finally roused, thrusting Sonny in front of him. "No, I'm fine, really. And of course I've seen twins before." He smiled, hoping to hold them at bay. "My father's a twin," he added truthfully, recalling his Uncle Trace, another useless second son who had missed inheriting the right to run Whittington, Inc. by a mere four minutes.

This revelation, however, failed to deter the twins from their appointed mission.

"If you'll step aside, Miss Sonny," Luke said, "we'll take this character off your hands."

"Oh, by all means," she replied, moving to her left. Turning Terry over to the twins' ministrations was one way of keeping him at Cara Mountain.

Each of them grabbed an arm. "Scrawny, ain't he, sister," Henry said, squeezing his biceps.

"Ouch!"

"Downright puny," Luke replied, ignoring Trace's protest as she applied the squeeze test to his other arm. "We best waste no more time gettin' this sorry specimen of a man to the doc's."

"If we don't die laughin' first," Henry said. Laughing, anyway, the sisters each bent to grab a leg.

Trace's eyes bugged at Sonny. "Do something!"

"Now be a good patient, Terry," she said, patting him on the back.

As the twins moved to lift him, he tried to struggle free of their hold, but to no avail. He, Trace Whittington, a man who religiously avoided humiliation, was being trotted off like the featured guest at a pig pull, and by women, no less. Over his shoulder, he glared at Sonny. "I'll get you for this, I swear," he said, making a mental note to return to the mountain with her, and this time, throw her off.

Sucking in her lips, her eyes merry, Sonny turned her palms up in a gesture of helplessness. Then her gaze went to her father as he entered the room.

"I'm glad to see you're up—you'll pardon the pun—young man," Chapin said, grinning. "Though I'm not so sure you should be on your feet just yet."

Trace blinked, once. "As you can plainly see, I'm not."

Stepping closer, Chapin examined each of Trace's eyes. "That *was* a nasty blow you took."

"That's what me and Henry's been trying to tell him, Mr. Chapin," Luke said. "You can't play fast and loose with them thwacks on the pate, less you want to end up crack-brained."

"Exactly," Chapin said, standing beside Sonny and putting his arm around her shoulders. "Carry on, ladies. You'll pardon—"

"I know," Trace said, "the pun." Despite his contortions and demands that he be put down, Henry and Luke held him fast as they paraded him to the door. His only option was to glare threats of reprisal at Sonny, who, he saw, was too busy crumpling with laughter to notice them.

"Just look at his eyes, sister," Henry said. "Wild as my Emory's when he gets in a lovin' way."

"Not near as allurin', though, sister," Luke replied.

Henry came to a dead halt. She yanked her side of Trace away from her sister. "And how would you be knowin' that, Luke Barrow?"

Luke yanked her side back. "That's for me to know and you to find out, Henry Barrow."

Henry gave such a hard tug on Trace's left side he swore she was trying to make a wish on him. "Cain't I have nothin'a my own?" she cried.

Trace glanced at Luke Barrow. If the murderous glint in her eye wasn't intimidating her sister, it was certainly scaring the hell out of him. She tightened her grip, striking him with sheer terror. "Ladies, please! Drawing and quartering was outlawed centuries ago."

Henry put her face in his. "Well, it'd go a whole lot easier on you if you'd stopped squirmin', son. Come on, sister, let's get this boy to the doc's before he has a conniption."

Sonny raced ahead into the office. "I'll be glad to get the door," she said, giving Trace an infuriating grin.

He refused to add to her amusement and so he resigned himself to going out the door in ignominy. At least he'd go out in one piece. Besides, it probably wouldn't hurt to have his head examined—in more ways than one. And anyway, his stomach was beginning to feel a little queasy.

But as the Barrow twins started out the office door and he glimpsed the man just now stepping from a four-by-four, Trace went from queasy to sicker than Emory was going to feel after Henry got home. That row would look like a prayer meeting compared to the one that was about to erupt in the next fifteen seconds.

That was about how long Trace figured it would take for Cortland Rockwell III to recognize him and for Sonny to find out she'd fallen for a man who didn't exist.

4

AFTER MAKING CERTAIN that neither Sonny nor her hench-women, the Barrow twins, lurked outside his cabin, Trace stepped into twilight on Cara Mountain. Gazing up at the crest where the world had fallen into his arms that morning, he saw it gleam brilliant in the last bright light of day. But below, emerald leaves and the gem tones of young wild-flowers were muted to gray, and slivers of chill air sliced through the afternoon's store of warmth. If the mountain could talk, he thought, it might tell him the secret of ex-isting in both light and shadow, as he was now. It might tell him where the truth lay, nearer to the crest or at the base or somewhere in between. No, there was no in-between. Sonny and every good thing she made him feel was the top of the mountain. Below was nothing but a life he'd grown weary of living, a life he wanted the chance to climb up from.

He'd nearly lost that chance when Cort Rockwell had appeared outside Chapin's office. Before Cort could spot him, Trace had convinced Henry and Luke that his break-fast was about to reverse its course, whereupon, they re-versed theirs. They deposited him in Chapin's bathroom. He'd locked himself in, gauged the size of the window in relation to his frame, and quickly despaired of escaping. But the rattling of the doorknob and the bellowing of the twins as they threatened to "come git him" propelled him through the narrow opening with urgent force.

On the way to his cabin he had gotten lost for nearly two hours. After passing the same covered swing three times, he finally took up its offer of rest and promptly sat on a wasp. Looking up as he removed the stinger from the back of his thigh and swearing that if he ever saw Sonny Chapin again he wouldn't be responsible for his actions, he had seen Sonny. And he hadn't been responsible for his actions, because the very sight of her long legs in tight jeans, the motion of her hips as she climbed the path he faced, the reds and golds rioting in her hair, aroused his body in ways he couldn't control. Yet she not only ignited his desire for her, but the desire to fight for her, for something better. For the best.

Ducking behind the trunk of an oak, he had watched as she continued to climb, carrying a tray covered with a checked cloth. After she had returned down the path moments later without the tray, Trace tracked her climb and found that it had led, as he had suspected, to his cabin. Inside, he found the tray containing hot chicken soup, an assortment of sandwiches and a note: "Henry and Luke are devastated. No man's ever run out on them before—at least not successfully." Then, "Coward."

The word might have been a right cross. Trace stood stunned, consoling himself that Sonny had only meant to tease the man she knew as Terry Wright. But he was inconsolable. She had used that word to describe the man she held in contempt, the man he really was. A man he no longer wanted to be. He had to find Cort. Either that or imprison himself in his cabin for fear of Cort's finding him first and blowing his cover. To avoid detection, he'd wait until dusk, then using the map of the mountain retreat Chapin had given him when he'd checked in, search for The Angler, the name of the cabin he'd overheard Chapin tell Cort would be his.

As the mountain went to silhouette, he found the cabin tucked deep in a cranny in its darkened face. The night air was cool, but far from necessitating the use of a fireplace. Still, smoke curled from the chimney. Trace could only conclude that Cort—not surprisingly—was entertaining a female guest. Although Trace had seen Cort with a number of beautiful women, he found the prospect of actually catching his friend in flagrante delicto utterly distasteful. Sowing wild oats as a bachelor he understood all too well. But any man who'd risk losing his wife and his home baffled and saddened him. Growing up in Palm Beach where divorce was a major industry, he'd seen too much of its wreckage, too many lives washed up on the sands like seashells, pretty but empty. Besides, he couldn't afford to compromise his suit against the baroness by getting mixed up in the media circus that would inevitably surround the divorce trial Cort was headed for.

What he could afford even less, though, was for Cort to give away his true identity to Sonny before he could prove to her—and to himself—that Trace Whittington wasn't a coward. As he approached the cabin door, he heard a woman's enchanting laughter, then as the door opened, saw its source step outside.

"Good night, Cort. I hope you sleep well," the woman called solicitously into the cabin.

"After what you just did to me? I'm exhausted."

"You know you'll come back for more," the woman replied. "You always do." Drawing the collar of her light jacket around her throat, she headed up the path.

Trace blocked her way. "Hello, Sonny," he said. He didn't know how he got the words out because his face, like his heart, had suddenly turned as hard as the rock looming above him. He should have guessed something fishier than the trout kept Cort coming back to Cara Mountain.

"Terry?" Sonny threw her arms around his neck, her smile sweeter than it had a right to be. "What are you doing here?"

He broke the circle of her hold. "Getting sense knocked into me."

Sonny gave him a puzzled look, then smiled again,

brightly. Too brightly, Trace thought. "I was just on my way to see you."

Trace's jaw flinched, but not his gaze. "You're a woman who gets around," he said, and as Sonny appeared to have no idea what he meant, he thought her performance remarkably convincing. She sighed and essayed another smile, this one striving for sincerity.

"I was worried about you."

When she raised her hand to the bump near Trace's temple, he caught her wrist. He was worried about him, too, because he couldn't remember ever feeling this jealous over a woman he barely knew. He couldn't remember feeling this jealous, period. Or this stupid. In the past five years he'd tangled with—and disentangled from—the most sophisticated women on two continents, sustaining not so much as a scratch to his pride. Until now, until this mountain nymph had worked her magic on him. Served him right for falling for the first woman who appeared to be genuine. He had to hand it to her, though. That line about believing in him, believing he was a man of conscience, was good. A complete lie, of course, but damn good. "I'm sure you have better things to do," he said, and releasing her arm, walked away.

"Terry!"

As he stalked toward the woods, into the comforting darkness, he marveled at just how good she was, at how that pained catch in her voice had nearly lured him into looking back at her.

"Come on, Terry!"

She ran after him and, clasping his hand in both of hers, fell into step beside him. Her touch might feel like liquid lightning, but he'd be damned if he'd be struck twice. "Terry, stop. Please!" Letting go of his hand, she came to a halt. "Where's your sense of humor?"

That did it. Turning, Trace stared at her in amazement. Not even the most jaded of his Gabrielles would have been so brazen as to suggest that not only shouldn't he be angry that she'd made a fool of him, he should be able to laugh at it. "Forgive me," he said mockingly, though he wasn't sure which of them he disdained more. "I must have left it in my other pants."

Spanning her waist with her hands, her elbows akimbo, Sonny stamped one foot in front of her. "You're certainly making a big deal of nothing, I must say. It's not as though there was any real harm done."

Eyes popping, Trace rocked back as though he'd been slapped. "It may be no big deal to you, but even where I come from any woman with a shred of self-respect would have the nominal decency to show a token of remorse."

"For heaven's sake, Terry. What does decency have to do with anything?" Spreading her arms, Sonny shrugged. "I admit I had a good time, but—"

"Of all the shameless—"

"Shameless?" Her eyes widening, Sonny made a defiant braid of her arms. "All right, so maybe things did get a bit out of hand."

"Ye-e-e-s," Trace said, his head nodding accusingly as he came toe-to-toe with her. "Dangerous things, hands."

Unfolding her arms, Sonny held her hands out. She looked first at the left, then the right, then at Trace. "What on earth are you talking about?"

Throwing back his head, Trace uttered a derisive laugh. "Oh, you're good. I mean you're the best I've ever run across, and that's saying something."

"Thank you," Sonny said with a generous dose of sarcasm. "But I still haven't the faintest idea what my hands have to do with my letting the Barrow twins have their way with you this afternoon!"

Trace propped his hands on his hips and gazed bitterly at Sonny. "Oh, you don't. You..." Losing their hold, his hands plummeted to his sides. "The Barrow twins?"

Sonny shook her head as if to shake the disconnected pieces of the preceding conversation into place. "That's what you're so upset about, isn't it? The way I let Henry and Luke womanhandle you?'' Pulling a leaf from an over-hanging branch, she turned away and stepped into the moonlight. ''I'm sorry, Terry,'' she said, looking at him over her shoulder. ''I know I should have stopped them when they started playing tug-of-war with you, but if you could have seen your face...''

''Forget the Barrow twins.'' He fixed a prosecutor's stare on her. ''What about Cort?''

''Cort?'' Sonny whipped around. ''Do you know him?''

Trace's jaw hinged up and down, then finally emitted sound. ''I heard you call that name at the cabin door.''

''I suppose I did,'' Sonny said. ''What about Cort Rogers?''

Rogers? Well, for one thing, Trace thought, the rat is using an alias, after all, so he must be afraid some big-mouth bass might report his whereabouts—and his who-withs—to his wife. ''Friend of yours?''

''In a way. He's one of Dad's regulars and always asks for me whenever he comes up here.'' Sonny's gaze narrowed, then she laughed and added, ''Actually we have more of a sporting relationship than a friendship.''

Picturing the dignified, white-haired Edward Chapin, Trace's mind reeled. ''And your father doesn't mind?''

''Of course not.'' Sonny blinked uncomprehendingly. ''Why would he?''

Trace's mouth went slack with disillusionment. Apparently the middle-class morality he'd secretly admired all these years—albeit from afar—had been nothing more than a myth. ''I can't imagine,'' he muttered.

Sonny cocked her head to one side. ''Look, Terry, I don't know what you think you overheard back there, but—''

''Hey, Sonny!'' Cort's voice rang from the cabin as his silhouette appeared in the doorway. ''You forgot your fifty bucks!''

''Oh, my God!'' Turning his back to the cabin and on Sonny, Trace buried his head in his hands. How many shattered illusions could a man withstand?

"I'll be right—" An abrupt silence sawed off Sonny's reply to Cort. "Oh!"

At her scream, Trace spun around, only to take a dirt ball in his openmouthed face. As he blinked bits of dust from his eyes, he felt something move across the surface of his tongue. Gagging, he clutched his throat. "Pleh. Pleh, pleh." A small black beetle landed briefly in his cupped palm before he shook it off in violent disgust, saving his fury for Sonny. "What did you do that for?"

"Oh, I don't know," she whispered angrily, flinging her hands in the air. "Maybe because you thought I was a hooker!"

"I never said that," Trace replied, equally incensed.

"But you sure as hell made an Olympic broad jump to that conclusion!" Sonny's voice was a quiet rasp of rage.

"Look, I've seen you in action and it's a safe bet you're not a personal trainer or a dance instructor. What else *could* I conclude?"

Sonny's chin quivered, whether from pain or anger or both, Trace couldn't tell. "Did you ever think of backgammon?"

Inserting his forefinger in his ear, Trace dislodged a wad of earth. "Come again? I thought you said backgammon."

Sonny thrust her face in Trace's. "That's exactly what I said, you— Why am I whispering? YOU GUTTER-MINDED SIGN IGNORER!"

Anger, Trace decided, reeling back from the blast. The chin quiver had definitely been a sign of anger. And as he watched Sonny gather another mound of dirt, pack it, then advance on him with her arm cocked, he saw yet another sign, one he had no intention of ignoring. He ducked behind a tree.

"Come out from behind there, you coward!"

Maybe he *was* a coward, Trace thought, but he wasn't crazy. "Not until you put that clay fastball down," he called. "I don't mind the mud facial, but I have to draw the line at insects. I'm watching my protein intake."

"O-o-oh!"

Hearing an explosion like a tiny land mine, Trace took one step from behind the tree, then another that turned into a lurch when Sonny grabbed him by his jacket.

"I'm going to say this just once, so listen up," she said in the most menacingly soft tones Trace had ever heard. "Cort Rogers comes here to fish and, if I happen to be here at the same time, to play backgammon, a game at which I am exceptionally good. The *only* game at which I'm, I'm…"

Abruptly Sonny turned away, the barely perceptible racking of her shoulders betraying her emotions.

Shoving his hands into his pockets, Trace hung his head. When Sonny had thrown that dirt ball in his face, she had insulted the dirt. "Oh, Sonny, don't cry. Please." He took her by the shoulders but she jerked from his grasp. He sighed, paused a moment, then said, "I have an idea. I'll laugh about the Barrow twins and then you can laugh about this little…misunderstanding, and we'll call it even. How about it?"

Sonny inhaled deeply, her back stiffening, but said nothing.

"Ha, ha, ha." Trace walked around Sonny, facing her and breaking into knee-slapping laughter. "See, I'm laughing." This time the mud on his face resulted from her icy stare rather than her pitching arm. "Come on, Sonny. As you said before, no real harm was done."

With her arms clutched about her, Sonny toed the ground, then looked up at Trace. "You're right, Terry. There's no harm done because I'm never going to see you again."

Trace gazed deeply into her eyes and knew she meant it. He also knew, for the second time in his life, what it felt like to lose what he most wanted, though he felt far worse now than when he had failed at his attempted takeover of Whittington. What he still didn't know was how to show his heartache. "Fine with me," he said, folding his arms and taking a wide stance.

Sonny lifted her chin. "Fine," she said. As she turned to leave, Cort's voice brought her back around.

"Sonny, there you are. You forgot—"

Trace went from desolation to panic faster than his Ferrari went from zero to sixty. He couldn't let Cort get a look at him. He had just one hope of averting certain—and permanent—disaster, of losing Sonny forever. Taking her in his arms and crushing her to him, he kissed her as though his life depended on that kiss. As a matter of fact, he thought, it did.

MADMAN! FISTING her right hand, Sonny pummeled Trace's back while pushing against his chest with her left. She might as well have been trying to move Cara Mountain. If he thought all he had to do to change her mind was to sweep her into his arms and kiss her like some silent-screen ham, he had another think coming.

"Oh, sorry," she heard Cort say. "Didn't know you were meeting someone. I'll just hang on to your winnings for you. Well, ciao."

"Mmmmm!" Her mouth otherwise occupied, Sonny wordlessly voiced her objections to Cort's leaving her alone with this…this maniac. Behind Trace's back she waved Cort closer. From her right eye she saw a perplexed expression overcome his tanned face, but at least he was staying put. There had to be some way to signal him that she was being held against her will…held in the strongest, surest arms she'd ever felt.

Cort looked behind him. "Well, I'll see you tomorrow, Sonny. Remember, you promised to give me a chance to win my money back."

"Mmmmm!" As she saw Cort back away, she protested more loudly, scudding her heels across the ground. Thank God—that tactic brought him to a halt. But it also made Terry press his lips more fiercely to hers, lips that were full and warm and— And no way was she going to let them erase the memory of how their insufferable owner had insulted her!

His tongue, however, was altogether another matter. It had so expertly claimed the recesses of her mouth, nothing else could explain the sudden genuflection of her knees. As Terry responded, lifting her off the ground, she wrapped her legs around his hips. Plunging her fingers through his hair, she kissed him back, hard, twining her tongue with his.

"Sonny?" Cort stepped closer. "You okay?"

Raising her hand, she waved him off.

When Cort had returned to his cabin, Trace set Sonny on her feet. And not a minute too soon. Her tongue was an exquisite instrument of torture, capable of making a grown man weep or, at the very least, of causing him visible embarrassment. Cupping her face, he traced her arousingly sweet and swollen lips with his thumb. Appalling to think he'd not only made her cry, he'd damn near let her get away. "Can you ever forgive me?"

Sonny's lids shuttered several times before she brought Trace's face into focus. "Forgive you? What for?"

Bringing her forehead to his lips, Trace gently kissed it. Oh, what he'd come so close to losing, the chance to know this angel. He already loved her, but he had so much to learn about her, and he could hardly wait to begin. "For not having invited you to have dinner with me when I first saw you fifteen minutes ago. It just so happens I have two thick filets and a fair bottle of wine in my cabin."

Sonny fell captive to a vision of the two of them sitting at a candlelit table, sipping ruby wine, holding hands, disclosing secrets of the heart they'd never shared with anyone else. Suddenly she found herself wondering what kind of razor and shaving cream he used and how they would look in her medicine cabinet. "I'll overlook it this time. Just don't let it happen again." She smiled softly. "Please don't ever let it happen again."

Trace circled her waist with his arm and headed them up the path that wended through the woods to his cabin. They hadn't gone far when they saw a beam of light through the trees.

"Sonny?"

"Dad?" Looking up at Trace, Sonny slipped from his hold and hurried toward the figure emerging from the woods, a flashlight in his hand. "What's wrong?"

"Nothing, nothing." Edward Chapin patted his daughter's arm, allaying her fears. "I just thought you'd like to know you had a phone call." He slid a glance at Trace, then bending close to Sonny, lowered his voice. "From New York."

Taking her cue from the arching of her father's brows, Sonny left with him, promising to meet Trace for dinner in half an hour.

Two hours later Trace blew out the candles on the table, put the cork back in the Beaujolais and returned the filets to the refrigerator. Grabbing his jacket, he strode out the door and into the night, bent on finding Sonny and getting down on one knee if that's what it took to keep her from getting away from him again. But first he had to alert Cort Rockwell.

"FOR THE LAST TIME, Sonny, listen to reason. Don't go!"

Shuffling to a halt opposite her father's desk, Sonny faced him. "My mind's made up, Dad," she said, then scooped the keys to his Blazer from atop a stack of Cara Mountain brochures. "Are you going to drive me or shall I leave the truck at the airport?"

Shaking his head, Chapin took the keys and headed out to the four-by-four. Climbing in beside Sonny, he gave her a look of intense consternation. "What about Terry Wright?"

Sonny felt her stomach drop, but forced herself to stare detachedly out the windshield. "What about him?"

"Believe me, honey, I didn't need a flashlight back there

in the woods," Chapin said, jerking his thumb in their direction. "All I had to do to find you was follow the sparks you and he were giving off."

Sonny looked at him. "Was it really that obvious?"

"Let's just say I'm glad there weren't any heat-seeking missiles in the area."

Sonny glanced down, a slightly embarrassed smile on her lips. Catching sight of her mother's wedding band on her right hand, she fingered it reverently. It symbolized not only the complete devotion her parents had had to each other, but everything she had ever dreamed of sharing with the man she would spend her life with. A love that had no beginning, no end. Strange, but whether or not what she felt for Terry was love, it was certainly something she sensed had always existed and always would. When she was in the circle of his arms, she felt as though she were in the center of all things, where time had no meaning, yet forever-after was possible. Possible with a man she had only just met, yet had always known. How could she even consider walking out on him now?

Difficult as it was, she had no choice. Unless she took advantage of this godsend of a chance to finish off the Whittingtons—and the baroness, too—she'd never be really free to love Terry. Every minute they were together she'd feel like a cheat, and when they were apart, she'd worry he might discover his lover was the woman he'd called a parasite. No, when she came to him, the Whittingtons, the baroness and *Celebrity* magazine would be well behind her. And if by some chance Terry ever did find out about her "titled" past, she'd make him understand she had written those stories for the sole purpose of avenging her father, hanging the marauder who had plundered his business. Besides, by the time he did find out, she'd have moved on and become the writer he said she had the talent to be.

"Dad, please try to understand," she said, laying her hand over her father's. "You want me to quit writing for *Celebrity,* don't you? Well, so do I, and I'll never have a better opportunity than this one to get the information I need to finish what I started there and go on with my career. I'm doing this for you, Dad, and for me *and* for Terry. So, to answer your question, I've left a note in his cabin explaining I was called away on urgent business and asking him to wait for me, here, or wherever it is he's from."

"And if he doesn't?"

Sonny let out a long sigh. Withdrawing her hand, she huddled in her seat. "Then I can only assume those sparks you saw were nothing more than cheap backyard fireworks."

Wordlessly Chapin started the truck. After several miles he breached the tense silence. "I thought you said your editor ordered you to stay away from the Whittingtons. What made him change his mind?"

"He didn't," she replied. "He doesn't know about the invitation from Diana Whittington Baird to 'commune' with her family at their Palm Beach estate. Before I left, I asked one of my office pals to monitor my mail and calls and let me know if anything even remotely connected to the Whittingtons came in."

"Office pal, huh?" Chapin gave Sonny a skeptical look. "How much did it cost you?"

"Dad, I'm surprised at you," Sonny said. "It's not like you to be so cynical."

"How much?"

Propping her feet on the dash, Sonny slunk lower in her seat. "Oh, all right. Fifty. And another fifty not to tell Jack." She bolted upright, pointing a finger at her father. "But it will be worth every cent, Dad. You'll see."

"I'm not so sure." As their descent steepened, Chapin geared down. "What about this lawsuit Trace Whittington is threatening against you and the magazine?"

"His sister must have talked him out of it," she replied. "In her letter she said her family wanted to pursue the cause of peace on earth and goodwill toward personkind. I know I may be taking a lot for granted, but I assume that includes reporters.''

"Still, it sounds to me as though you're getting in way over your head, Sonora."

Sonny paused, as she always did when her father called her by her full name. Then, shrugging and spreading her hands, she said, "What's the worst that can happen? Jack could refuse to print the juicy story I'm going to get out of a Whittington soul-baring—or whatever it is that family substitutes for souls. But I won't have any trouble selling it elsewhere."

"He *could* fire you."

"I was going to quit eventually, anyway." Sonny shook her head. "No, Dad, the only party that stands to lose in all this is the Whittington family." She wrapped her arms about her and smiled, too smugly, she knew. But she couldn't help it. "And is the party ever over for them."

SHINING HIS FLASHLIGHT on the door of Cort's cabin, Trace knocked. "Cort," he called in a loud whisper. But he heard no response from inside the still and darkened cabin, no movement. Pressing the thumb latch, he found the door unlocked and let himself in. Except for embers in the hearth, the main room was black as a cave. Trace shined the light about it, trying to find his way to the bedroom where he assumed Cort was well into an X-rated dream. As he quietly closed the door behind him and stepped into the room, he felt a tap on his shoulder. With a start he whipped around and suddenly the room exploded with sky-rockets.

"Ow!" Holding his hands over the eye that had just been punched shut, he careened over the back of the sofa, then somersaulted to the floor. As he hauled himself to his feet, a body hurled itself at him, flattening him like a duck in an arcade. Before he could protest, two hands were at his throat, beating his head against the floor as though it were something to stamp out roaches. "You maniac," he managed to squeeze from his constricted windpipe. "It's me!"

Apparently "me" wasn't sufficient identification, nor did Cort recognize his strangled voice, because he went on dribbling Trace's head.

Reaching between Cort's hands, Trace broke his choke hold, then threw him off. "It's me, Tr— Umph!" Man, he hated head butts in the stomach. Clamping Cort's biceps, he rolled across the floor with the man, taking out a table, a lamp and a vase, which emptied its cold contents on Trace's head. Enraged now, he hoisted Cort to his feet and held him off with his left hand, cocking his right fist back. "Freeze or I'll break your nose like I did when you sailed my boat *and* my date to Grand Cayman. And this time I won't pay to have it fixed!"

"Buddy!" Cort wrapped Trace in a back-slapping hug.

"Get away from me, you moron," Trace said, shoving Cort and rubbing his neck. "You damn near killed me."

Cort switched on the light over the kitchenette table. "I heard somebody skulking around outside. I thought you were an intruder or, worse, a private detective." His eyes narrowed. "What are you staring at?"

Trace ran his one-eyed gaze over Cort's powder blue pajamas printed with items he was seeing but not believing. "I always wondered whether the world's greatest lover slept in the nude or wore his teddy-bear jammies. Now I know."

"Hey, my wife gave me these," Cort said, looking down at them. "They're kind of a joke. When she wants to make love, she calls me…" Clearing his throat, he padded to the sink. "How about a cup of coffee?"

Grinning, Trace went to the freezer and withdrew some ice for an ice pack. "She calls you her what? Her teddy bear? Teddy Ruxpin? No, I know. Cuddly Duddly!" He broke into laughter so raucous he discovered that in addition to a sore eye, he had a bruised rib.

"Yeah? Well, that's how much you know," Cort said, filling the coffeepot. "Cuddly Duddly was a dog."

Trace laughed harder, wincing between bursts.

"Just what the hell are you doing here, anyway, Whittington?"

Sitting at the table, Trace began at the beginning, with Sonny dropping into his arms that morning. By the time he finished, the coffee had run out.

"Let me get this straight," Cort said. "Since you met Sonny Chapin less than twenty-four hours ago, you fell down a mountain, got a concussion and your bare toes crushed, was attacked by two lusty amazons—"

"The Barrow twins weren't lusting after me."

"I understand that," Cort said. "Emory, I believe, is the lucky man. Still, you had to lock yourself in the bathroom and crawl out the window. Then you got lost in the woods for two hours, during which time a wasp bit you in the behind. When you saw Sonny outside my cabin earlier tonight, she smacked you in the face with a beetle-infested dirt ball, then you came back here and got a black eye and a bruised rib." He took a breath. "And you're in love with the woman?"

"Right," Trace said. "You have a problem with that?"

Cort wiped his hand over his mouth. "Oh, no. Just thought I'd ask." He folded his hands on the table. "And now you plan to fight Arthur for control of Whittington Enterprises so Sonny won't think you're a moral coward."

"Right."

"Wrong!" Cort slapped the table. "Look, Trace, do you realize what you'll be risking? You could blow your wad, your whole damn inheritance." He paused as a grim thought obviously entered his mind. "My God, you'll have to work!"

Trace smiled, oddly touched by Cort's concern. "All I know is I'll be risking a lot more if I don't try. A man is nothing without his self-respect."

"Well, I wouldn't go that far," Cort replied, blinking twice. "I don't have any self-respect and—"

"And no offense, pal, but what *are* you?"

Puzzling, Cort looked away. Then brightening, he returned his gaze to Trace. "My wife's Pooh Bear?"

Groaning, Trace lowered his forehead to the table.

"I see your point," Cort said.

Trace popped up. "Then you'll promise that if you see Sonny and me together, you'll act as though you don't know me?"

"After the transformation I've seen in you tonight," Cort began, "I won't have to act." Rising, he stretched and said he needed his beauty rest, then added, "By the way, how's your father?"

Trace pressed his hands to the tabletop and slowly rose. "What do you mean?"

"Well, just before I left Palm Beach I'd heard he'd been taken to the hospital. Didn't anybody get in touch with you?"

"Nobody knows where I am," Trace replied, panic rising inside him.

Twenty minutes later he was packed and ready to head home. Having paid Chapin cash in advance for a week's rental of the cabin, all that was left was to tell Sonny. But at nearly two in the morning, he decided to write a note, instead, promising he'd find her on Cara Mountain or at the end of the earth, and asking her to wait. As he affixed the note to the refrigerator door, he saw one addressed to him. When he'd read of Sonny's own emergency, he carefully folded the note and tucked it into his wallet. He knew he'd want to read it again and again. *She* had asked *him* to wait, and she had signed her name with love.

5

OUTSIDE THE TONY BOUTIQUE, palm fronds swayed against a cerulean sky, and the sun shone its brilliance on Palm Beach's designer-labeled Worth Avenue. Inside, Sonny stood before a gilt-framed full-length antique mirror, considering a natural linen pantsuit by Versace, umber silk shell by Guy Laroche and complementary print scarf by Longchamp. Simple but elegant and three times as expensive as it looked, the ensemble was exactly what the Whittingtons would expect a baroness to wear. But did she dare buy it?

As she took another turn before the mirror, she reminded herself of one unassailable fact. The success of her plan to ferret Whittington secrets and expose them to the financial world depended on her ability to convince the family and its intimates—anyone of whom could be her informant, Madame X—that she was one of them, one of the privileged few, and could be trusted. Besides, she hadn't even bothered packing the grubbies she'd taken to the mountain and had nothing other than her current outfit to wear. Exhaling a long-held breath, she turned to the sales assistant. "I'll take it," she said, adding the Italian shoes with matching bag and the oversize costume pin and earrings that bespoke the flare for style without pretension she imagined the baroness had.

After changing back into her own pedestrian jeans, cotton T-shirt and blazer, she delved into her sole bag, a travel tote, for her credit card. Technically it wasn't her personal card but one the magazine had issued to her influential pseudonym, Sophia Oleska, for expenses. Of course the expenses her employer had in mind were the usual travel and entertainment costs incurred while interviewing press-hungry celebs who were too preoccupied with projecting their own images to notice hers. Even the discharged valets and maids she met in dark bistros paid her no personal attention. They only wanted to use her for their revenge, revealing for her column that Count So-and-So painted his toenails or Princess Such-and-Such was into studded-leather bedroom wear.

But for sojourning as the baroness with one of the most celebrated families on Florida's celebrated Gold Coast, she needed to costume herself for everything from a sumptuous dinner to tennis to sailing on a yacht. Besides, it would be weeks before the bills arrived at the office and Jack screamed for her head. Presenting her card, she signed for her purchase.

The sales assistant, herself a study in elegance, painstakingly wrapped the items then hastened to open the door for Sonny. "May I say I enjoy your column, Baroness. And certainly appreciate your patronage. Please do come back and see us."

Pausing, Sonny met the clerk's deferential gaze. "Oh, I couldn't think of doing anything but." *Just seeing you, that is.*

Despite the reminder that penury was her natural state, as Sonny stepped into the sea-kissed air, she happily noted she had just passed herself off as nobility to a woman who ought to know a baroness from a barmaid. Carrying off her masquerade might be easier than she had imagined. After all, she had made a career of studying the Whittingtons' social set, of knowing it well enough to write about it as an insider. As she shopped her way up the avenue, adding Louis Vuitton luggage to her plunder, she increasingly felt as though she really did belong. So much so that when an enchanting hibiscus-covered archway beckoned her to explore the narrow "via" that lay beyond, she did so without hesitation.

The small street opened onto a courtyard. In the center a botanical garden bloomed with exotic flowers, luring her deeper into an enclosure of small shops—a jeweler, parfumerie, children's clothier, art gallery. A Spanish café nestled in the corner, its outdoor tables clustered beneath an awning and its patrons serenaded by a guitarist. Sonny inhaled deeply of the rare atmosphere, thankful it was free. She doubted she could charge much more before setting off alarms at the credit-card company. In fact, given that the Whittingtons weren't expecting her until tomorrow, she probably ought to pick up the luggage she'd left at the shop and get a cab back to the mainland, where she could find a cheap place to lodge for the night. Reluctantly she turned to leave. But noticing the day spa tucked discreetly in another corner of the courtyard, she stopped to examine her fingernails, perennially stubby from years at the keyboard. No matter how much Louis Vuitton she set on the Whittingtons' doorstep or how posh her attire when she arrived, her nails would surely expose her charade. No self-respecting baroness, even a journalistic one, would do her own typing.

Three hours later Sonny's fingers were tipped with acrylic and given a French polish. Her skin had also been detoxified with extracts from plants found in an underwater cave off the Greek Isles, and her face, which the cosmetician had excitedly declared a "virgin canvas," had been freshly painted. Sitting in the "hair therapist's" chair, with her back to the mirror, she asked Maurice how much longer it would be before he had finished with her. He'd been at it so long she suspected he was waiting for new growth to accomplish his vision.

Abruptly he ceased operations. "Young woman, if it's miracles you want, you'll find the Church of Bethesda by the Sea not far from here!" Slamming his comb on the counter, he folded his arms and turned his back to her.

Sonny shifted her gaze from side to side. The other therapists and their patients were obviously too engrossed in their own sessions to notice the breakdown in hers. Never having had her hair "counseled" before, she had no idea what to do next, other than to turn to the mirror for a self-analysis of her condition.

Which, as it turned out, *was* miraculous. For a solid minute she gaped at the tousle-haired, dark-lashed, pouty-mouthed sophisticate who stared back at her, a woman who would command admiring gazes from the Costa del Sol to Cancun and everywhere in between. Slowly her glistening lips formed a smile. "Hello-o-o, Baroness."

Maurice glanced at her over his shoulder, then stalked off. But Sonny was too mesmerized by her own transformation to notice. She returned to the dressing room, asked the attendant for her things, then stuffing her own clothes into a bag, donned one of the outfits she had bought for Sophia. Emerging into the small reception area with her cache, including the palette of products that had re-created her face, she saw Maurice and a statuesque blonde in consultation. The instant they spotted her, they broke off. No doubt, she had set the progress of hair healing back a decade.

She approached the pair, credit card in hand, expecting a word of reproach from Maurice, a word like "peasant!" Instead, he perplexed her, giving her a formal bow before disappearing into the salon. The woman introduced herself as Ilsa, the spa manager.

"I hope you will excuse Maurice's rudeness, Baroness."

Oh, now I get it, Sonny thought. A peasant's just deserts is an insult to a baroness. Looking down her nose, she said, "My good woman, there's simply no excuse for it."

Ilsa appeared stunned, then wetting her lips, said, "I'm sure you understand how temperamental these artists can be."

"I thought he was a therapist," Sonny replied dryly.

Obviously on edge, the woman laughed too loudly. "Well, therapy is as much art as science, isn't it."

Sonny squared her shoulders. "Is it?" To her delight she saw Ilsa swallow hard.

"But of course, he had no way of knowing." Abruptly she tore Sonny's bill in two. "I hope you will consider the matter closed. And whenever you're in Palm Beach—"

"I know," Sonny said, grateful for the freebie but nevertheless quite tired of being bowed and scraped to. It wasn't healthy. "Come back and see you."

Visibly relieved, Ilsa smiled. "May I ask, where is the baroness staying?"

Sonny supposed Ilsa meant to send roses of remorse. That was fine with her, though she would have felt better if she believed the woman would do the same for plain Sonny Chapin. "I'm a guest of the Whittingtons."

"Very good. I've taken the liberty of calling a car that will take you there."

Sonny's stomach lurched. She hadn't expected that. But what had she to fear? All she had to do was tell the truth. "That won't be necessary," she said. "Arthur and dear Lotti aren't expecting me until tomorrow."

"I see."

As Sonny turned to the door, she blew back her bangs in relief.

"In that case," Ilsa said, "I'll instruct the driver to take you to the Breakers."

"Huh?" Sonny turned, her thickly lined eyes bugging.

"That's where you're stopping, isn't it?"

Of course that was where she *would* be stopping if she really *was* a baroness. "But...but I wouldn't want to put your driver to any trouble. I have some purchases to pick up." She hurried to the door.

"It won't be any trouble at all," Ilsa replied, following her. "Charles will be glad to make as many stops as you wish. Consider him at your disposal."

Before Sonny could stammer out an excuse, the woman

withdrew. A frantic assistant had announced that Maurice was so despondent he was threatening to turn in his smock.

An hour later, after the driver had retrieved her new luggage and announced her arrival to the doorman, Sonny was ensconced in a luxurious Italianate suite in one of the most famous hotels in the world. And one of the most expensive. Even if Trace Whittington didn't sue her, the magazine surely would. As she gazed at the waves breaking on the beach and the vastness of the ocean beyond, she recalled her father's warning that she could be getting in over her head. She wondered if she ought to have paid it more heed.

But she also recalled the feel of Terry's arms around her, of his warm lips devouring hers and the look of contempt in his smoky eyes when he had called the Baroness Oleska a parasite. Turning from the window, she caught her reflection in a mirror above the marble mantel.

"Hang in there, kid. Just a few more days, then it's goodby-y-ye, Baroness."

TRACE LAY ON HIS BED, staring at the ceiling, his hands cupped behind his head. Below him the house buzzed like a hive in preparation for the "baroness." If only it *were* a wasps' nest, he thought. Then with any luck she'd be deathly allergic to the stings. But after his frantic drive back from North Carolina, which Cort in a remarkable show of decency had volunteered to share with him, he was too exhausted to further indulge in venomous fantasies about the woman. Besides, he had too many more important matters on his mind.

His father, for one. After repeatedly failing to reach anyone in Palm Beach, Trace had been relieved to arrive there and discover that A.W. had only stepped barefoot on a shard of glass and taken a few stitches. No, Trace thought. More than relieved, he'd been overjoyed. Trace had always loved his father, had always known he would be devastated should anything happen to him. But until now he had never considered that he might have disappointed A.W. when he skipped out after losing his battle with Arthur for the chairmanship of Whittington Enterprises. The man had never uttered a critical word to him. Actually not one for idle chatter, he'd uttered few words of any kind to his son. Nevertheless Trace now felt an urgent need to do his old man proud.

Which brought him to the second matter troubling him. Turning on his side, he picked up Whittington, Inc.'s annual report, which he had just finished reading. Each page had confirmed his worst fears about Arthur's gross mismanagement of the firm. Worse, the notice of the annual stockholders' meeting that had accompanied the report not only proposed the renewal of Arthur's contract but a massive increase in his compensation and benefits package. Trace knew that unless he came up with a plan before the meeting, the board of directors would rubber-stamp the proposal and perpetuate Arthur's reign of error. The only hope he, Trace, had of stopping them was to wage a proxy battle, but the odds he could prevail were at best slim. Besides, a campaign to win stockholder proxies would consume every minute of his waking life.

And that brought him to the third and most pressing matter. Sonny. How long would she wait for him? Even if he could stage a coup at the next shareholders' meeting, it was six weeks away. A man could lose a lifetime in six weeks.

Hearing a knock at his door, Trace answered it. "I thought the doctor told you to stay off that foot," he said as he let his father into the room.

"I've never followed a doctor's advice before," A.W. said, "and I see no reason to start now. May I come in?"

Perplexed as to the reason for this unexpected visit—unexpected for more than twenty years—Trace nevertheless stepped back to allow his father to enter. Anticipating an explanation, he followed as A.W., cane in hand, limped to the chair by the window, sat and gazed down at the pool. Trace wondered if his father was recalling those midnight swims they'd shared long ago.

"I assume you'll be present at our reception for the baroness this evening," A.W. said, turning at last to his son.

"That harpy? You can't be serious." Trace gave a snort, mostly at himself for hoping A.W. might have come calling just to spend time with him or maybe to say he appreciated the way his younger son had come rushing back from North Carolina to his side. When would he learn? He wasn't needed around here. Abruptly, his gaze flew back to his father. "Wait a minute, *our* reception? Don't tell me *you* plan to be there."

"I wouldn't miss it for all the paint your mother's bought in the forty years we've been married."

"Why?" Trace plopped onto his bed. "Why would you lower yourself to sitting at the same table with that scandalmongering phony?"

A.W. propped his foot on the ottoman. "You're right, of course. She's no more a baroness than I'm a NASA astronomer." He folded his hands on his still-taught abdomen. "But she is a guest in our home, where, I'm told, charity begins. Call off your lawsuit, Trace, at least while she's staying with us."

Shaking his head as he laughed to himself, Trace rose and walked to the window. "Now I get it," he said. "My lovely, meddling, world-saving sister, Mother Diana, put the arm on you." Rubbing the back of his neck, he turned to his father. "I don't blame you, A.W. She *is* your daughter, God help you. But you can tell Diana that if she wants to practice brotherly love, she can practice by leaving me out of this nutty scheme of hers!" Stalking across the room to his closet, he rummaged for his favorite deck shoes. When the baroness arrived, he'd be miles out at sea.

"Interesting you should mention fraternity," A.W. said. "Your new brother-in-law will be attending with Diana, of course. I just thought you'd like to welcome Brian to the family."

Slipping on his shoes, Trace paused. "You have a point. If I wait much longer, he may not be family."

"I wouldn't bet on it this time."

"I'll take that bet," Trace replied, pulling a loose striped T-shirt over his bare chest.

"Still a gambling man, I see." Lowering his foot, A.W. rose. His gaze wandered to the report on Trace's bed, then settled on his son. "I can't say I'm entirely displeased."

Trace's eyes narrowed in puzzlement. "What's that supposed to mean?"

On his way toward the door, A.W. halted, leaned on his cane and looked his son in the eye. "When you figure it out, be sure to let me know. And don't forget to change before you come down."

"Which I won't," Trace replied. "Besides, I thought the idea was for the baroness to see us as we really are."

"Yes, I suppose it was," A.W. said, shrugging a small concession. "But who knows? *We* might even see each other as we really are."

Thoroughly confounded, Trace watched his father hobble from the room. All he knew for certain was that if a completely and outrageously false persona was good enough for the baroness, it was good enough for him.

AT PRECISELY SEVEN that evening, Baroness Sophia Oleska, dressed in a daring little black sheathe of open-work lace over *peau de soie* and with straps so thin they should have been called vermicelli rather than spaghetti, gasped. The limousine that had called for her at the Breakers had just swung into the driveway of the Whittington estate off South Ocean Boulevard. To know the history of the Mediterranean villa concealed from tourists by tall privacy hedges and lush trees was one thing. To see it loom into view was breathtaking.

Casa Carlotta had been built by Palm Beach's premier architect, Addison Mizner, in the 1920s. Arthur Whittington IV renamed it for his bride more than thirty years later. With its red-tile roof, Moorish windows and staircase tower made graceful by a rising open arcade, it might have been conjured up by a genie. As the car stopped before the tile steps leading to the double-door entrance and the driver helped the baroness to alight, she made a wish of her own. She wished she wouldn't throw up.

Behind those doors, Sonny knew, lay her future. A new career, a new life with a man she'd fallen in love with on Cara Mountain. A man she had abruptly left there. And all she had to do to secure that future was to convince forty or so of the most sophisticated people in the world, including her sworn enemies, that she really was a baroness. Her one hope was that Madame X, whoever she was, would be in attendance and help her to gain acceptance.

As she climbed the steps, the doors swung open. A petite mature woman who nevertheless appeared impish with her bobbed hair and twinkling blue eyes stepped outside. She wore a simple sheath covered with iridescent blue sequins, though Sonny thought she looked more like a little girl playing dress-up. A man using a cane followed. He was silver-haired, trim, dapper in formal wear. His chin was cleft and his eyes were a deep blue-gray. No doubt, Sonny had seen photographs of A. W. and Lotti Whittington, but something about A.W. was strangely familiar to her, as though she had actually met him before. Her nerves, apparently, were rattling her mind. Cautioning herself to get a grip, she greeted her host and hostess.

"You have no idea how we've looked forward to meeting you, Baroness," Lotti said. "I must say you're much younger than I had imagined."

At closer range, Sonny saw that the sparkle in Carlotta Whittington's eyes came from a diamond-hard probing intellect. Despite her eccentricities, Lotti Whittington was no fool. Sonny mustered every ounce of bravado. "Really? Perhaps that's because I bear such an old family name."

As the two women stared each other down, A.W. offered Sonny his arm. "You're certainly lovelier than *I* had imagined, Baroness. Shall we go in and meet the rest of the clan?"

Entering the great hall, Sonny's breath caught again at the sheer size of it, the magnificent spiral staircase, the rich tapestries, the glittering chandelier. It looked more like a ballroom, which she surmised it might later serve as, given the ensemble playing softly in one corner. Thank God her parents, who had loved ballroom dancing, had taught her the basics. As she gazed up at the vaulted Baroque-style ceiling, she suddenly and surprisingly felt sorry for the Whittingtons. How tragic it would be to lose such a glorious and historic work of architecture. Yet, if they did, they had only themselves to blame, A.W. for ceding the family business to Arthur and Arthur for his stupidity and greed. But the worst of the lot had to be Trace. He could save both Whittington, Inc. and Casa Carlotta, but he was too self-indulgent, too cowardly to try.

Lowering her gaze, Sonny saw a stiff-looking couple— a couple looking like two stiffs, actually—beswarmed by a pair of small boys and a girl committing a prosecutable level of physical violence on one another. Ah, she thought, this charming tableau could only be Arthur Whittington V and his family. As the man kissed her hand, the introduction A.W. gave him proved her correct. She was still shivering when Arthur presented his wife, Lydia.

The Woman of No Body Fat gave Sonny a hand icier than her husband's. "Your grace."

"I'm not an archbishop, Mrs. Whittington," Sonny said with withering hauteur. *But if I were, I'd see what I could do about having you raised from the dead.*

"Baroness?"

Sonny turned to her right. A stunning redhead approached wrapped in a metallic gold dress that revealed every luscious curve. She could only be the much married—

"Diana Baird," the woman said, extending a hand that Sonny found surprisingly warm. But after shaking hands with Arthur and Lydia, she would have found the touch of a salamander warm. Then, too, Diana's reputation for hot-bloodedness was legendary. "I'm so pleased you came," she said softly. "I just know you and I are kindred spirits. You wouldn't have accepted my invitation if we weren't."

I accepted your invitation to do you and your whole family of cuckoos, cutthroats and cowards in, Sonny thought. "The pleasure, I assure you, is all mine."

Diana smiled with obvious delight. "Baroness, I'd like you to meet my husband, Brian."

As Diana stepped aside, Sonny's heart stopped. Brian Baird was blond, handsome—and in a wheelchair. Diana pushed the chair forward, then helped her husband to lock it in place. Bracing himself, he struggled to a half-standing position.

"Please don't," Sonny said.

Brian gave her the bravest and proudest smile she'd ever seen. "I've been practicing for days," he said, "but this is the best I've done yet. If Diana had told me you were so beautiful, Baroness, I'd be running laps by now."

"I didn't tell you what the baroness looked like, beloved, because I didn't know," Diana said to her husband as she helped him to resettle himself.

"And would you have told me if you had?" Brian gazed up at his wife.

"No." Clasping his hand, Diana smiled at Sonny. "I *am* incredibly jealous, but I'm working on it."

Sonny saw husband and wife exchange a look she had often seen her parents bestow on one another. Adoration.

As the other guests began to arrive and Sonny took her place in the reception line, two questions nagged her nearly to distraction. Where was Trace Whittington? Not that she was surprised he hadn't the courage to meet her face-to-face. And could an obviously reformed Diana Whittington Baird be Madame X?

As she developed that theory, a man appeared before her, a man who sent shock waves through her body, causing her legs to wobble like towers in an earthquake. In the next ten seconds everyone in the room would know she was a fraud. What was Cort Rogers doing here?

Presenting himself as Cortland Rockwell III, she soon discovered. Of course, he was Trace Whittington's childhood pal and a notorious womanizer. Not that he'd ever made advances toward her, nor had she ever known him to bring a woman to Cara Mountain. But he hadn't used an alias for no reason.

"I don't know you and you've never seen me before in your life," he whispered, taking her hand. Then, louder, "I'm honored to meet you, Baroness." And giving her a wink, he introduced his wife, Maura.

Perhaps it was his having concealed his true identity from her, or maybe it was his wink, but Sonny was now convinced that Cort was Madame X. Her father must have let it slip that his daughter wrote for *Celebrity* and Cort had taken it from there. But why? What stake did he have in the Whittington fortunes? Before the evening was over, she had to get him alone.

The opportunity arose sooner than she had expected. Now that all the guests had arrived and the champagne flowed, the band went into full swing. A.W. pardoned himself for not asking her to dance, designating Arthur his stand-in. Sonny cringed, but she was saved from a fate worse than death when Cort swept her from Arthur's cold grip.

"I must say, you're equally attractive in tight jeans or the little black number you're wearing tonight."

"You phony," Sonny murmured.

Cort gave her a wicked smile and a twirl. "Now if that isn't the baroness calling the kettle black." Pressing her close, he whispered in her ear, "I have something to tell you, Sonny. You're not going to like it."

"Why don't you try me?" She laughed. "Madame X."

Cort pulled back. "Madame X? I'm talking about Trace."

"Trace Whittington?" Sonny whirled as Cort moved her away from a flamboyant fox-trotter. "What about—"

"Hello, everyone!" A deep male voice called from the grand staircase.

Cort abruptly stopped dancing. "And now if you'll excuse me, Baroness," he said, handing her off to a young, tanned and tuxedoed passerby. "I tend to faint at the sight of blood."

Stunned and confused, Sonny watched Cort depart, then slowly turned toward the man descending the stairs. She could see nothing more than his Italian loafers and that the feet in them were bare.

"So sorry I'm late," he said, putting the pommel of his fist to a yawn, "but I had a rather exhausting night."

"Yes, probably at Au Bar," Sonny's companion called out, referring, she knew, to one of the hottest nightspots in the area.

"Please," the man who had now come into her view said with a mock frown. "Not in front of the baroness. Where is she?"

Despite his looking like a young Douglas Fairbanks, Jr. in white linen pants, navy blue blazer with gold-crested breast pocket, striped shirt and red-white-and-gold silk ascot, Sonny instantly recognized the man gazing over the heads of the guests. The man who was looking for her.

Her mouth dropped open, her voice escaping on the breath of a whisper. "Terry!"

6

ADJUSTING HIS ASCOT, Trace descended the stairs. He lifted a glass of champagne from a tray borne by a passing waiter, downed it, then replaced it with another. If he was going to get through this charade, he'd be damned if he'd do it stone-cold sober. He'd also be damned if he'd see the sun set on Lake Worth without giving the "baroness" exactly what she expected of him. He didn't care how old she was or how many jowls she had, he'd turn on the playboy charm she claimed he'd used to seduce every socialite under fifty on two shores. And turn it on her. The woman needed a lesson.

Fortunately for the teacher she was far from jowly. As he made his way toward the woman who had been pointed out to him, he noted the bare, slender and lovely back turned to him, the narrow waist, enticingly delineated hips and legs that wouldn't quit. They reminded him of Sonny's legs, or what he imagined Sonny's legs looked like. He couldn't wait to get back to Cara Mountain and find out, though he wouldn't care if her knees knocked and her ankles were thick as tree stumps. All he knew was that *she* had given *him* legs to stand on once again, and he was crazy about her. And the sooner he dispatched this viperous fraud from their midst, the sooner he could concentrate on seizing his future with the only woman who had ever believed him capable of seizing anything but the moment. By the time he finished with the "baroness," that phony would be spilling the secrets of her soul to him as though he were her confessor. Only he wouldn't be bound by the silence of the confessional. He'd feel no shame in threatening to turn the tables on her, to see how she'd like having her every quirk, foible and failing—and those of her family—exposed to the public. Wouldn't her devoted readers just love to know that Sophia Oleska hailed not from Prague but from Paducah or Pittsburgh, where she was born Sophy Oles or Susie O'Leary or—

"Sonny Chapin?" The name formed inaudibly on Trace's lips as Diana presented him to their honored guest. Little did his sister know she had introduced him to the death of his newborn hopes and dreams.

Sonny's heart was pounding so violently she barely heard Diana's introduction. But the man who stood before her needed no introduction. He was the man who had just destroyed the most precious of her ideals, leaving her as empty as the crystal flute slipping from her benumbed hand. She heard it explode into tiny irreparable fragments.

"I'm sorry," she said flatly, her gaze never wavering from Trace's. *Sorry it wasn't your heart. But then, you haven't any.* He had known all along of course that she was the baroness. Cort, perhaps in a moment of guilt over his role as Madame X or simply tiring of it, had told him with the hope of arranging an "understanding" between his friend and his friend's enemy. But true to his nature, Trace had most likely decided it would be easier and a lot more fun to seduce Sonny Chapin for revenge than to work out an understanding. He wasn't only a coward, he was the worst kind of cad. And she'd be damned if she'd let him think he had gotten away with his scheme. She laughed dismissively. "How clumsy of me."

"And how deliberate," Trace retorted. She had known all along of course who he was. She must have seen him checking in at Cara Mountain and recognized him from that old prep-school photograph filed away in that evil mind of hers, though he couldn't see how. Not even Lotti had recognized him in that picture when she'd come across it recently. Or worse, maybe that paparazzo in Paris had rescued his film before Trace snatched his camera and tossed it into the Seine. The vermin had probably gone straight to where he knew he'd get top dollar for it—to *Celebrity* and the "baroness." He tasted bile, imagining how she must have salivated at the prospect of humiliating him. But he'd be damned for eternity if he'd let her know she had succeeded in playing him for the utter fool he was.

As the band went Latin, striking up a tango, and staff arrived to remove the broken crystal, he deposited his own glass and swept her into the dance of dueling passions. "But you didn't really think you'd fooled me, did you? Or that I really believed it was an accident that you fell into my arms on that mountain?" *That you made me fall in love with you.*

"Of course not." Sonny smiled as if smiles could kill. "And you didn't think I fell for that line about my being sweet?"

Trace jerked her into a sidestep, pressing his cheek to hers and wishing he'd kept his usual growth of bristle. "And you didn't think I believed that bit about my being a man of conscience?"

As Trace dipped her, Sonny laughed in his face. "And you didn't think I wasn't sick to my stomach every time you kissed me?"

Trace lowered her dangerously nearer the floor, grinning malevolently from above. "And you didn't think it wasn't making me sicker to do it?"

"And you don't think," Sonny began, gritting her teeth, "that your hand on my back right now doesn't feel like slime?"

Briefly considering letting her go then and there as he should have done on that damned mountain, Trace, instead, whipped her upright. He crushed her to him. "A leech ought to know about slime."

Sonny clamped her fingers on the back of his neck, and brought her lips close to his. "A coward ought to know about leeching off the fortunes his grandfather and father made.''

His nostrils flaring, Trace danced Sonny in the opposite direction, meeting Diana as she tangoed toward them in the arms of a guest. Her expression lit up with glee. ''I just knew that you two only had to meet to adore each other,'' she said as she passed them.

Sonny had no choice but to look into Trace's eyes as he executed a wrap, holding her back to his chest. ''Well, what are you waiting for?'' she asked. ''Why don't you expose me?''

Trace lowered his gaze several inches to the cleavage he remembered all too well pressing his cheek to. ''That dress you're almost wearing seems to have already begun that task.'' Pushing on the small of her back, he unwrapped her, then pulled her against him, holding one arm behind her.

''One I'm sure you'd like to complete,'' Sonny retorted, grinding her toe on his. One corner of his eye flinched, but he refused to acknowledge the pain. He merely released her arm, then performing an elegant lift, deposited her behind him and joined them back to back. ''You know very well that's why you followed me here,'' Sonny said, snarling over her shoulder. ''To humiliate me.''

Whipping around to face her, he grasped her waist and raised their clasped hands above her head. ''Don't flatter yourself that I arrange my life around you. As much as I'd like nothing better than to watch you squirm, I couldn't blow the whistle on you without humiliating my family, especially Diana. Palm Beach would never stop laughing at how she'd been taken in by an impostor, and not a particularly convincing one at that.'' Closing the gap between them, he added, ''But consider yourself warned. Not all the Whittingtons are as witless, to use your deft term, as my dear sister.''

Obviously not, Sonny thought, comprehending him. He was telling her that as of this moment she could abandon any notions she had of unearthing sordid facts or scandal for her column. Except for Diana, they were all on their guards. And Sonny was suddenly in even deeper water. The only hope she had of justifying her outrageous expenses to Jack was to break a story—a story he had forbidden her to chase—that would sell so many copies of *Celebrity* he could truthfully tell the publisher it had come cheap.

"At least I'm getting a free vacation out of all this," she said, following his stride around the room and speculating that memories of sun-drenched beaches and balmy breezes would come in handy after she'd been jailed for defrauding the magazine. "What are you getting?"

Lunging first to her right, then to her left, Trace peered into her eyes, eyes he once thought could see into his soul. He knew now they had never seen anything in him but a boost in circulation. "Bored."

Sonny searched the eyes of the man she once thought she'd fight for, fight beside. Hell, he wasn't even worth fighting with. "In that case, why not stick around? You might learn a thing or two." *From your sister, for example. She may not be a brain surgeon, but at least she knows what the human heart is for.*

"Yes," Trace said, looking down at Sonny with feigned regard. "I'd love to learn how you plan to keep me from eventually exposing the baroness."

Sonny stole a glance around her at the glitterati before whom he had earlier refused to embarrass his sister. "I don't understand."

"If you'll recall, I never said I wouldn't reveal your scam to my friends in Europe." Trace moved his hips against hers, keeping time to the pulsing beat. "When the word filters back here that the beautiful people on the continent have been exposing their soiled silks to a con artist for a coveted mention in her column, Diana will become just one more hapless victim, instead of a laughingstock. Palm Beach society will close ranks around her, and I wouldn't be surprised if you couldn't get a job writing obituaries."

Though the music was hot, Sonny's blood turned to ice. Trace had the power to ruin her career, and what was more, he had no scruples standing in his way. No conscience whatsoever. All she had was the will to honor a vow to see the Whittingtons brought down, a vow that had just become an obsession. "Maybe. But before I hang up my word processor, I intend to inflict a lot of damage. Perhaps *you* ought to stay around to try to stop *me*."

Trace leveraged Sonny into another, deeper dip. "I'm sure I would find that very entertain—" Seeing her breasts rising before him like two magnificent snowy peaks, Trace lifted her face into view. "Entertaining. But I'm afraid I couldn't afford the cover charge." Abruptly returning her to vertical, he cut her with his gaze. "I don't have what it takes to spend one more minute in your presence."

As the music swelled, Sonny raised her hand to his cheek, then thought better of allowing him to cause her any more pain than he already had. "Let me go before my knee forgets itself."

The music ended. Trace released his hold of her back, though his eyes continued to dance with mockery as he lifted her hand to his lips. "Goodbye, Baroness. Parting is such sweet—"

Sonny snatched her hand away. "Yes, and it was never—" thrusting her face in his, she spit her final word "—sweeter!" Fueled with heartache, anger and the desperate need to put as much space as possible between her body and his, she turned away.

And was immediately jerked back around. "What are you doing? I said let go of me!"

Trace raised his palms. "Look, Baroness, no hands."

Giving him a furious once-over, Sonny started another turn. Again she boomeranged, her abdomen colliding with his and nearly knocking the breath out of her.

The bandleader, apparently thinking Trace and Sonny still wanted to tango, struck up his musicians. Sonny glanced at the crowd gathering around them. "Great.

Thanks to you, the band thinks we're putting on a ballroom-dance exhibition and everyone is staring at us.''

"Thanks to me?" Hearing his shout echo, Trace lowered his voice. "Look, Baroness, dancing with you is like dancing with a Clydesdale. If I had to choose between another tango with you and the rack, you can just imagine which torture I'd choose. And gladly!''

Unable to find words to express her outrage, Sonny stamped her feet. When the other dancers applauded, she realized they thought she'd been doing flamenco steps and rolled her eyes. "Trace Whittington, if you don't release me this instant, I will accuse you of something that would embarrass even you, and at the top of my voice.''

"Believe me, I'd love nothing better than to let you go,'' Trace replied. "If I had a brain in my head, I would have done just that when I found you on that mountain.''

"Fine.'' Fixing him with a slit-eyed gaze, Sonny filled her lungs. "But Mr. Whittington! You *must* be the same man I just happened to see in that bedroom with the Barrow twins. You look exactly like him!'' She addressed the crowd. "There they were on either side of him, you see, and—''

The great hall echoed with laughter. Even the band broke off playing and substituted wolf whistles for Latin guitars. Seething, Trace tore to his left. Sonny, inexplicably but undeniably stuck to him, stumbled after, tripping his foot. He lurched, she followed, bending backward over his left arm. He bent over her. The more they tried to right themselves, the more they tangled.

"I always said nobody could tango like Trace,'' a sultry-voiced woman called out to the delight of the onlookers.

"Yes, who taught you to dance, Trace?'' a man asked. "Hulk Hogan?''

"Two out of three falls,'' another said. "I'll put a thousand on the baroness.''

As the laughter became howls, Trace lifted Sonny, their midriffs joined, and carried her past the band. "Play!'' he shouted at the gaping musicians, who launched into "You Are the Wind Beneath My Wings," inciting the spectators to hilarity. Cursing colorfully in French, he set Sonny down beneath an arch leading to the library, as far from the view of the dancers as possible.

Tucking in his chin, he peered between their joined midsections. "I think I see the problem."

Sonny lowered her own gaze. "Oh, now look at what you've done!"

"What *I've* done?"

"I suppose that's not your stupid button caught in my lace?"

"No, your stupid lace snagged my button."

They glared at each other, then in unison, attacked the imbedded brass button.

"Stop it!" Sonny slapped his hands way. "You'll tear the dress."

"The dress wouldn't get torn if you'd stand still."

"Even if I stood still, my skin would keep crawling."

Propping his hands on his waist, Trace stared at the ceiling and began counting to ten. He only got as far as three before he dug in and ripped the button from his jacket. "There, now your skin and my life can return to normal."

"Exactly," Sonny said, throwing the button, which he avoided, at his face. "As Deborah Kerr said to Cary Grant, I'll go my way—" with her left hand, she indicated a straight and narrow path "—and you can go yours." Making a snaking motion with her right hand, she turned in the opposite direction.

Seizing her by the shoulders, Trace turned her back around. "Just one question, Baroness."

"It wouldn't be what's a nice girl like me doing in a place like this, would it?"

"No-o-o..." Trace cast a nervous glance at a passing couple. "It's more like, are you by any chance wearing a black strapless bra?"

Sonny's eyes squinted her disgust. "That's all you ever think about, isn't it?"

"Sometimes more than others," he replied, blocking her path as she attempted to go around him. "Now about this bra... Would it be mostly netting except for several strategically placed flowers?"

Sonny's mouth dropped. "Don't you dare move!" Lifting her brows, she glanced down her nose at the glittering strap detached from her dress, at the right side of the bodice flapping over her breast. Covering it, she raised a frantic gaze to Trace. "Get me out of here!"

"There you go again, mixing signals," Trace said, flinging his hands in the air. "Now which is it to be, stay or go?"

"You can't resist, can you?" Sonny was so blind with loathing she nearly missed seeing the butler approach. She dodged to her right, pulling Trace along as her shield. "This is payback for the dirt ball and the beetle, isn't it?"

The butler signaled the band to stop, then cleared his throat. "Dinner is served."

"No, I'm afraid *that* is," Trace said, propelling her toward the other guests who were filing past them on their way to the loggia. "You're about to be treated to one of Lotti's low-fat feasts. I hope you like recycled paper *à la grecque*."

As he marched her forward, Sonny resisted, clutching her bodice with both hands. "Look, I can't go out there like this. I'm going to have to make myself decent first."

Grabbing her by the crook of the arm, Trace turned her sharply toward him. "You don't have that much time."

Sonny wished she'd slapped him when she'd had the chance, but on second thought, she doubted she could have stung him as hard as she wanted to, as hard as he had her. She was still smarting when Diana appeared asking if Trace wasn't going to escort their lovely guest in to dinner. Soon Sonny was following her sympathetic hostess up the curving staircase to the suite that had been prepared for her.

Diana informed her that one of the maids had unpacked her things, then asked if Sonny wanted her to wait while she changed. When the baroness "commanded" her to rejoin her other guests, Diana thanked her, saying she would see that Trace ushered her to the loggia.

"Please, don't trouble him," Sonny said, removing a lilac-beaded gown from a closet that was bigger than her New York apartment.

"Oh, but I love troubling my brothers," Diana replied, rushing to zip up Sonny's gown. "I think trouble encourages spiritual growth, though it doesn't seem to be doing much for Arthur. What do you think?"

"Well, I—"

"Besides, I hope I'm not being too forward when I tell you, Sophia—you don't mind if I call you Sophia, do you?—that I've never seen Trace look at any woman the way he looks at you."

Not surprising, Sonny thought. *I'm the only woman Trace Whittington wants to destroy.*

"And," she murmured, collapsing onto the bed after Diana had left, "he's succeeding."

DAMN IT. There was no way he could afford to let her out of his sight, Trace thought as he paced the great hall, waiting for her to come down. The more he saw of the "baroness," the less he recalled of Sonny Chapin. As long as the face of an enemy was before him, he felt safe. But the instant "Sophia" disappeared upstairs, he began to relive every moment with Sonny on Cara Mountain. He felt her melting in his arms and her kisses making him strong and her words of faith, bold. "Lying words," he muttered, removing from his breast pocket the note he had kept close to his heart, the one she had left him on the mountain. The one signed, "Love." He tore it into pieces, but his satisfaction was fleeting. He realized that destroying all evidence of her deceit was the last thing he needed to do. The memory of how tall and proud she'd made him feel was still so powerful, that unless he dwelled on her deceit, looked for it in those prevaricating eyes, he might fall victim to her spell a second time.

Hearing footsteps, he gazed at the top of the stairs. *That's right,* he thought, watching Sonny descend step by step. *Come closer and ease my pain. Let me despise you. And those red eyes! How thoughtful of you to bring me a sign that you were laughing so hard up there you cried.* He met her at the bottom and offered his arm. "Shall we, Baroness?"

Twining her arm with his, Sonny walked beside him through the main parlor and onto the expansive loggia on the east side of the mansion. On the many tables, candles flickered in the lush breeze wafting from the ocean. Gulls sang to the rhythm of the waves. Far across the lawn, a graceful blue heron, gently spotlighted, perched on the edge of a reflecting pool. She had never seen anything so romantic. And she had never believed less in romance.

Having to sit across from Trace throughout dinner only reinforced her disillusionment. Each meeting of their eyes was a replay of the one that had rocked her to her core less than an hour ago, when she recognized that the man she loved and the man she loathed were one and the same. The more she thought about it, the more insane the whole situation became. She'd have run from the table screaming before the salad course had been served if it hadn't been for Brian Baird, seated to her left. She learned he had suffered a spinal injury in a motorcycle accident several months ago, but that his doctors were hopeful that with therapy, he'd regain at least partial use of his legs. Before long, Sonny became convinced that he had more than enough optimism for himself, for the wife he clearly adored and for the entire human race. What a wonderful subject he'd make for a story, she thought, and how she'd love to write it—as Sonny Chapin.

Watching Sonny converse with Brian, Trace fumed. She was cool and brilliant, like a diamond, and just as hard.

While he kept reliving the shock of discovering he'd fallen in love with the woman who had trashed him on two continents and in four languages, she was obviously enjoying herself. She was also getting to know his new brother-in-law well, maybe too well. Certainly better than he did.

Trace had met Brian for the first time less than an hour ago. After Diana had taken Sonny upstairs to change, she had dragged him out to the loggia to meet the latest love of her life. He had found it strange that the man was already seated at the table, ahead of the other guests. And not only hadn't he risen to shake Trace's hand—which wouldn't necessarily have outraged Miss Manners—he hadn't stood later, when the ladies had arrived. While ignorance of the social graces certainly wasn't the most objectionable trait he'd ever encountered in one of Diana's husbands, he did have his concerns about Brian Baird. What was he telling Sonny that held her so rapt, and more disturbingly, would it appear in her next column? Was Brian more than just another fortune hunter? Was he the Baroness Oleska's informant? Perhaps he ought to get to know his brother-in-law better, and quickly.

"So, Brian," Trace began, interrupting Baird's tête-à-tête with the Barracuda Oleska. "What do you say we play a few sets of tennis at the club tomorrow?"

Instantly Trace felt the sharp tips of arrowlike stares, and Sonny's was dipped in poison. She was looking at him as though he had just suggested he and Brian spend a fun-filled afternoon pulling the wings off butterflies. What the hell was going on?

Breaching the fraught silence, Brian laughed. "Sure, then we can finish up with a round of golf."

Hearing the others laugh, Trace returned to trying to figure out if the puff on his plate was squash soufflé or orange-colored egg whites. Whatever the joke was, he wasn't in on it, which had become the story of his life since Sonny had dropped into it.

Although the others were laughing along with Brian,

who had generously chosen to diffuse the tension, Sonny could not. She'd had all of Trace Whittington she could stand. Rising and fixing him with a cutting stare, she flung her napkin onto her plate. "If you'll excuse me, I'm afraid I'm not feeling very well. It's been a very long and exhausting day."

Like hell, Trace thought as he rose, along with the other men, except for Brian. She had made it clear there was nothing wrong with her that his absence wouldn't cure. "If you'll excuse me, as well," he said, flinging his own napkin down. "My day is just beginning."

Leaving their stunned dinner companions behind, Trace went his way and Sonny went hers.

THE GUESTS HAD ALL GONE, Sonny knew, pacing her room. But even in this house, embellished with accents from Mediterranean churches and now as hushed, she couldn't sleep. Trace had been cruel to deceive her, cruel to seduce her to satisfy his petty spite. But there was cruelty and then there was the unspeakable. Not even Brian's gracious response had induced her to regard Trace's unutterable meanness as forgivable. How could she ever have thought she had seen things in those dusky blue eyes that obviously weren't there, things like honor, integrity, courage? Obviously she could no longer trust her own judgment. But what was really driving her up these tapestried walls was the memory of how her body had betrayed her, how it had surrendered to his touch. Suddenly she felt violated.

Pulling on her robe, she slipped downstairs and made her way to the French doors opening onto the loggia. As she reached for the handles, she paused, thinking she might set off alarms, then saw that one of the doors was slightly ajar. She stepped through. The loggia, swimming pool and gardens were softly illuminated, but beyond them, beyond the palatial lawn, the ocean sprawled, vast, dark and strangely inviting. Sonny heeded its call, navigating the thick lawn to the stone steps that led down to the shallow beach. There, she paused, listening to the surf wash over the sands. She wished it could cleanse her of the horrible sickening memory of how she had responded to the kisses of that vile man. The worst of it all was that she wasn't thinking only of how she had reacted on Cara Mountain. Lifting her gaze to the stars, she bared her soul to their light and confessed that even tonight, while she and Trace were dancing, she felt a physical attraction to him that belied her moral revulsion. Without doubt he was the most dangerous man she had ever met. And she had to get as far away from him as possible. Before the sun broke over the dark horizon facing her.

Turning, Sonny gasped with fright. She couldn't see the face of the man who stood before her, but his imposing build, the one she had once foolishly thought was a workingman's, was all too familiar.

"Are you out here all alone?" he asked.

7

"INCREDIBLE," SONNY SAID, staring up at the mammoth telescope belonging to the man she had understandably mistaken for Trace—his father. "I thought telescopes only came in two sizes, hobby store and Mount Palomar. I'm guessing that's where you'd have to go to find one larger than this."

"Actually I do know of a few," Arthur Whittington IV admitted, "but not many. We amateur astronomers—especially we males—are always comparing sizes." He gave her a wink.

Sonny looked away, both amused and mildly shocked. All through dinner, Whittington had barely spoken, and then only when his wife interrupted herself to ask, "Isn't that so, A.W.?" Far from rotely agreeing, he would always look directly into her eyes and reply with some variation of, "I've never known you to tell an untruth, Lotti dear." Sonny soon realized he wasn't a cold man, just extremely literal and self-contained, as though he lived most of his life on the inside. But here in the observatory he had tucked away in the most remote and private reach of his estate, he was quite different. Animated, easygoing. Even slightly naughty.

"Tell me something, Mr. Whittington," she said. "Do you really believe we all came from somewhere out there?" Sonny pointed at the dome of the observatory.

"Of course." Whittington pressed a button and the dome opened, revealing a starscape. "The stars and planets are our ancestors. We share a common source, a common chemistry." Cupping each palm, he rubbed his thumbs and fingers together. "We're made of the same stuff. It only stands to reason they have a lot to teach us about where we came from and who we really are."

As Whittington limped to the computer that guided his telescope around the galaxy, Sonny gazed up at the slice of night and pondered his remarks. Had she seen them in *Celebrity,* for example, she would have taken them as one more laughable proof that the congenitally rich were also inherently batty. But hearing them from a man who was clearly not six sandwiches short of a picnic as she had expected, and in this impressively scientific setting, she found them intriguing. She watched with fascination as the telescope tracked, fixing on the coordinates he had entered into the computer.

"How would you like to take a look at Gemini?" he asked, stepping away from the eyepiece and leaning both hands on his cane.

Eagerly Sonny took his place. She saw a cluster of lights, some larger than others, some brighter, but none of them lending her any clues to the secrets of the universe. She was disappointed. "Gemini is the sign of the twins, isn't it?"

"Castor and Pollux," Whittington replied. "They're the two largest stars in the upper left quadrant of your view. Do you see them?"

"Yes, I think so. One's a little lower and to the left of the other."

"That would be Pollux," he said, removing his light jacket. "He has a characteristic that distinguishes him from his twin, you know."

Glancing at Whittington, Sonny was momentarily taken aback. His chest was incandescing with the glow-in-the-dark Milky Way printed on his black T-shirt. Swallowing a chuckle, she took another look at the two stars. "They look the same to me."

Whittington typed data into the computer, expanding the

telescope's field of view, and guided Sonny to a star in the lower right portion of it. "That's Alhena. The ancient star-gazers thought of it as a mark on the feet of Pollux."

"Interesting," Sonny said. She turned to her host. "But frankly, Mr. Whittington, I haven't learned anything new about who I am." Remembering Terry's kiss, recalling Trace's cruelty, she looked away. "Who anybody is."

"That's where the stars come in, my dear Baroness." Whittington pointed to the sky chart on his monitor. "Take Pollux, for example. He's really a binary."

Sonny's brows shot up. "And does Mrs. Pollux know?"

Whittington laughed softly. "What I meant to say is that although he looks like a single star, he's really a double, two stars very close together. And Castor is really a triple-star system."

"If you're trying to tell me that people aren't always what they appear to be..." Walking beneath the telescope and joining him at the computer, Sonny peered at the dots on the screen. "I didn't need to look at the stars to learn that." *I only needed to see your son's face tonight.*

"True," Whittington said, clicking the keys and changing the configuration on the screen. The new one mapped the same constellation, but at a different time of the year. "But what studying the stars over a long period of time teaches you is that how they appear depends on where the Earth is in its orbit."

"In other words," Sonny said, turning her gaze on him, "where you're standing."

Whittington's only response was the shadow of a smile. Switching off the screen, he plunged them momentarily into darkness, except for the Milky Way radiating from his shirt. A glow of inscrutability bathed his expression, as though he were an alien sage, then vanished when he turned on the light.

"You've been kind to indulge me, Baroness," he said, pushing a button and sealing the dome. "But I'm afraid

I've imposed. I tend to forget that others don't share my enthusiasm for the heavens.''

Smiling, Sonny followed him from what he called the command center to the door. ''Please don't apologize. I liked the twins, especially Pollux.''

Whittington slipped his jacket back on. ''I'm glad. Truth be told, I suppose I'm partial to Gemini because I'm a twin myself.''

Sonny knew that. ''Terry'' had revealed it to the Barrow sisters.

''Trace is my brother's namesake, you know.''

She hadn't known that. Poor Uncle Trace. ''Are you and he identical?''

''Carbon copies.'' Gripping his cane in one hand and cupping Sonny's elbow in the other, he escorted her toward the door. ''Except for a large scar on the bottom of one of my brother's feet.''

''Alhena!''

Whittington appeared impressed. ''You learn quickly, Baroness. This particular mark was the result of a nasty accident Trace had on his bike when he was about ten. He was a clumsy child.'' Opening the door, he paused. ''Come to think of it, he's a clumsy adult.''

A man after my own heart, Sonny thought. Unfortunately, his nephew was after her hide. Sighing, she looked around and said, ''Thank you for sharing all this with me, Mr. Whittington. I—''

''Now that you've seen my equipment, I think you'd better call me A.W.'' Grinning, he took her by the hand and ushered her ahead of him. ''May I call you Sonny?''

Lurching to a halt and swallowing the brick in her throat, she turned to Whittington. ''How long have you known?''

''Since after-dinner drinks were served,'' he replied. ''I couldn't help noticing the looks you and Mr. Rockwell exchanged all evening. He's a remarkably bribable young man. I told him that unless he revealed your identity, I would inform his wife he had fallen desperately in love with her and hadn't once been unfaithful.''

Gaping, Sonny pressed her hand to her heart. "You mean he *wants* her to think he cheats?''

A.W. first swore her to secrecy. "It's a long story having to do with a scheme Cort's grandfather and Maura's grandmother cooked up to teach their grandchildren a few lessons.'' He placed a hand on her shoulder. "You're quite right to look bewildered, but I can assure you no one in Palm Beach would raise an eyebrow at the lengths to which people would go to to preserve their fortunes.''

To say she was bewildered was putting it mildly, Sonny thought. But there was one matter on which she was clear. "Cort may not be an adulterer,'' she said, "but I have every reason to believe he's a spy.''

Whittington's eyes narrowed. "What do you mean?''

"Using the name Madame X, he's been providing me with information about the Whittingtons and Whittington, Inc. for my column.''

A.W. appeared stunned. "I can't imagine why.''

Sonny thought for a moment. "Does the Rockwell family own Whittington stock?''

"Now that you mention it, I believe they do.''

"That's it, then!'' Sonny clasped his forearm with both hands. "He must be trying to drive down the price of the stock prior to a takeover attempt.''

"No!''

Sonny felt the sting of a double betrayal. First Trace, now Cort. Cort had been using her all along. He'd been manipulating her to enhance his own wealth, not to mention double-crossing Trace, though no one deserved it more. And what about A.W.? What was his angle?

"Now that you know who I really am,'' she asked, "what are you going to do?''

Opening the door for her, his expression solemn, he said, "Get some sleep.''

Right, and then what? Sonny wanted desperately to

know. She'd been stupid to tell Whittington about Cort's sending her information. Why should he believe she knew nothing of Cort's intentions? He could charge her with collusion, for heaven's sake, and she'd spend the rest of her life in jail. And her poor disgraced father would die of a broken heart.

This was all Trace's fault. If only he had accepted his responsibilities, wrested Whittington, Inc. from Arthur's control and made amends for what his brother had done to Chapin Industries, she wouldn't have written those columns. She wouldn't be looking at twenty years at hard labor in a prison laundry.

Closing her eyes, she stepped through the door and into something tall and hard and—

"Having a good time?" Trace asked, eyeing her peignoir.

Despicable.

"I SUPPOSE YOUR MOTHER'S convinced I've provided a feeding frenzy for trespassing alligators," Whittington said to his son. And to Sonny, "At least that's what my wife *claims* she worries about. Between you and me, I think she suspects that more than stargazing goes on in this place."

Trace didn't deny the implication that his mother had sent him after A.W. Sonny had humiliated him enough. She didn't need to know that, thanks to her, his round of the nightspots, always a salve for invisible wounds, had only made the pain worse. So bad, he hadn't been able to sleep. She didn't need to know that he'd had to go for a walk, keep moving, to get away from the memory of her on Cara Mountain. And the sting of her flaunting her deception in his own home. Seeing the light on in the observatory, he'd thought he would check on his father. Actually he'd thought of asking A.W. if he wanted to swim a few laps with him. But it appeared Sonny had other plans for his father.

"It certainly looks that way to me," Trace said so low

that only she could hear above the keys A.W. rattled as he locked the observatory. Then, more loudly, "A.W., I'll go on ahead and let Lotti know you're all right."

"No, I'll go, Trace. She won't relax, anyway, until she sets eyes on me. You walk the baroness back to the house." Before either Trace or Sonny could protest, Whittington was limping away at an amazing pace. "Take your time," he called over his shoulder. "It's a lovely night."

When he was out of earshot, Sonny rounded on Trace. "That was a horrible thing to insinuate about your father! He was merely showing me Castor and Pollux and—"

"And what were you showing him?"

She clenched her fists. "You filthy-minded—"

"If you're collecting Whittington men for your trophy case, you were wasting your time with A.W. He worships the drop cloths my mother walks on. But Arthur, now there's a challenge, even for you." Relaxing, Trace leaned against the observatory wall. "As far as we can tell, the only time a woman makes his blood thaw is when he thinks he can use her as a write-off."

"Well, this is one woman you can't write off," Sonny said, barely able to breathe through her indignation. "If I do end up pounding out obituaries, nothing will give me greater pleasure than to do a job on yours."

Wrapping her robe tightly around her, she stalked off into the darkness. Five yards out, she suddenly stopped and turned to Trace. "Are there really alligators around here?"

Sticking his hands in the pockets of his slacks and his tongue in his cheek, he strolled up to her. As far as he knew, while gators thrived in south Florida, one hadn't been spotted at Casa Carlotta since the Cuban missile crisis, when Lotti had sworn Castro sent it. "Oh, yes." He gave her a sidelong glance. "And other predators."

"Naturally," she shot back. "Where else would they find such juicy prey?"

Temporarily flummoxed, Trace watched her put distance between them, but he quickly closed the gap. "So you admit it! You came here to bury the hatchet, all right. In Whittington skulls!''

"Yes! And with damn good reason," she said, hurrying her pace. "Have you ever heard of a company called Chapin Industries?''

Trace grabbed her by the arm, turning her toward him. "As in Edward Chapin, your father? No.''

Sonny yanked her arm from his hold. "Dad spent his life building that company, and in less than a year your brother destroyed it. But of course you were too busy lapping up the good life to notice.''

Watching her scurry toward the pool, Trace stood paralyzed by the news she had just delivered. If it was true, he could understood why she'd been hell-bent on revenge. But *was* it true? Or was this just another of her elaborate lies?

"Sonny, wait!" He caught up with her as she hunkered behind the tall columnar shrubs surrounding the pool and on either side of its entrance.

"Shh!''

"No way! I want to talk about this. Now. I want to know—''

She clamped her hand over his mouth. "Look," she whispered, pointing at the pool.

Peering through the shrubbery, Trace saw his sister and her husband only a few feet away clinging to the side of the pool nearest them. "Diana hasn't gone swimming since she started wearing mascara, at least not voluntarily," he whispered back. Giving the scene closer scrutiny, his eyes widened. "Why the little devils. They're skinny-dipping.''

"I know," Sonny whispered back. "And that's not all they're doing.''

Trace chuckled. "I'm shocked. Shocked!''

Sonny glanced at him from the corner of her eye. "You're a sick man, you know that? She's doing therapy with him.''

"Sounds like what Diana would call it.''

Sonny gave a low groan of revulsion.

"Have you had enough for tonight, Bri?" Diana asked. Trace rolled his eyes.

"Yeah, but we'll do it again tomorrow," Brian replied.

Trace leaned close to Sonny. "At least she got herself a live one this time."

"Be quiet! You disgust me."

"But, Dee," Brian continued. "You have to promise me something. Promise me you'll complete those college applications." Laughing softly, he kissed his wife on the cheek. "I won't stay married to a dropout forever, you know."

"I promise," Diana said, returning his kiss on the mouth. "Come on, we'd better go. The air is starting to chill."

As Diana emerged first from the illuminated water, Trace and Sonny turned their backs at angles to the pool and to each other. After a few moments they resumed their eavesdropping. Diana, dressed in a short cover-up, was laying a large beach towel over Brian, who was already seated in his wheelchair.

"My God. No wonder..." Trace watched his sister wheel her husband around the far side of the house, where he guessed their car was parked. He looked at Sonny. "When I asked Brian to play tennis, you thought I *knew* he was disabled?"

Taking a deep breath at his audacity, Sonny folded her arms. "You really do think there's no situation you can't run away from or lie your way out of, don't you? Of course you knew he was disabled. He's your sister's husband, for the love of—"

"I only met him for the first time tonight, and he was already seated at the table."

"Right, and I suppose no one in your family told you about his condition before tonight, either."

"Before tonight," Trace said, "all I knew was his name and that Diana believed he was the true love of her life." Releasing a breath, he looked into the eyes he once thought shone with true love for him. "Now that I think about it, that's all two people who plan to spend the rest of their lives together really need to know about each other.''

Sonny's heart wrenched. That was what *she* had always believed, and for a brief moment on Cara Mountain she thought her belief had been confirmed. Strange that the item she had thought the easier of the two—knowing a man's name, his true identity—had proved the more difficult. Incredible it should have been the one to destroy her faith entirely. She wanted to cry but laughed, instead. ''Then I suggest you keep that in mind the next time you try passing yourself off as Terry Wright or whoever. Another woman might not find it as amusing as I did.''

Trace stood in awe of her colossal gall. ''You're amazing. You admit you tried to use me and actually enjoyed doing it, yet I offend your sensibilities with a cruelty I never intended.''

''You and I making sport of each other is one thing,'' Sonny said. ''But making that brave man the butt of your sick idea of a joke—''

''I know what you think of me, Baroness. I've read your column, remember? But even you...'' Trace turned away, his chest heaving with a stew of emotions. Why should he give a damn what she thought of him? He didn't care about the baroness, but plain Sonny Chapin, an illusory woman who was still so real he couldn't forget her. Even when he took her treacherous alter ego by the shoulders. ''You can't believe I'm capable of sinking that low.''

Staring at Trace, Sonny began seeing double. Terry was there, or rather the shadow of him, haunting her. And taunting her with the same false promise—that he was a man she could respect, a man whose battles she could fight as Diana had Brian's. All right, so he'd fooled her once. But never again. ''Can't I? If you hadn't needed me to carry out your childish revenge, I'm not so sure you would have risked your thin skin to get me down from that tree.''

''Please, let's not mince words at this late date,'' Trace said, flinging out his arms. ''You said it before, when you were plain Sonny Chapin. Why not say it again? Or did you need the cover of that charade to call me a coward to my face?''

Sonny gazed at that face. And she couldn't do it. She couldn't call him a coward and she had no idea why, when she believed in her bones there was no other word for a man who would abandon his family's fate to pirates like Arthur and Cort. But her bones weren't the part of her anatomy in command at the moment. How could she betray herself this way, feel so attracted to a man who was the antithesis of everything she thought a man ought to be? But for her own perverse reaction to the likeness of someone who never existed, she'd have no qualms about calling him a coward. ''Forgive me, but I find it hard to believe the infamously self-indulgent Trace Whittington would have taken time out from his pleasures to rescue me if he didn't know I was the baroness.''

I didn't know you were the baroness and I would have died for you. But I'd sooner rot in hell than let you know, Trace thought. ''Certainly I would have. I've never looked a gift female in the mouth, though from where I stood below you I was looking at—''

''Enough! I should have known,'' Sonny said. Either he'd been a brilliant actor up there on the mountain, or she was the most self-deluding woman ever born. She must have been hallucinating when she thought she'd seen a hint of Terry's sincerity in Trace's insufferably smug expression. ''I'm sure you'll be happy to know there's no part of my person you'll have to look at any longer. I'll be leaving first thing in the morning.''

Trace knew he should have been ecstatic. Discovering he wasn't only made him crankier. ''I'll see that a car calls to take you to the airport.''

''Don't bother.''

''It's no bother,'' he snapped. ''I just want to be sure you don't miss your plane.''

''I'd sooner miss winning the lottery.'' Turning on the

heels of her mules, then recovering from a wobble, Sonny clip-clopped toward the pool.

Trace watched her go, her satin robe streaming behind her like her satin hair. "Damn." She *was* beautiful and there had been a moment just now, when he'd looked into her eyes and had seen the ghost of Sonny's faith in him, he could have taken her into his arms and carried her back to Cara Mountain. Back to where they could be Terry and Sonny again, two ordinary people who just happened to meet and fall in love. One kind word from her, one shred of regard for him, and he would have done it, too. He might even have swallowed his pride and confessed he never knew until tonight that she was anyone but sweet, adorable Sonny Chapin. Fortunately she had made that impossible when she all but called him a coward.

At that moment, he decided, he'd never give her the satisfaction of calling him that. "Somehow, some way," he said as he tore off toward the beach, "I'll get control of Whittington, Inc."

Hearing a splash, Trace stopped and listened. Maybe A.W. had gone for a swim, after all. Not that it mattered, he thought, moving on. He had some serious thinking to do. Alone.

"Help!"

Trace halted, then deciding the cry he'd heard must have come from a restless gull, walked on.

"Trace!"

As far as Trace knew, he wasn't on a first-name basis with any gulls. Ripping off his jacket, shirt and ascot, he dashed back to the pool. "Sonny?"

"I can't—"

To his horror, Trace saw her thrashing and gulping water in a desperate attempt to stay afloat.

"Hold on!" Pulling off his loafers, Trace hurled himself into the pool and windmilled toward her.

But when he reached her, there was no her there. He treaded water and frantically scanned the area around him.

She was gone. Filling his lungs, he dived and burrowed to the bottom. It was empty, except for two sunken slippers. He gathered them, pushed off the floor, shot upward and broke through the lapping surface. Shaking his head and blinking his vision into focus, he saw...

Toes. Painted toes that led to slim ankles and long legs outlined by a clinging wet robe. From there, his gaze made the leap to the smirk on Sonny's face.

"The way I figured it, you'd had your fun and would just as soon be rid of me, permanently." She pushed a plastered strand of hair off her cheek. "So maybe you're not a complete coward."

Tossing the slippers behind him, Trace swam to the side and hauled himself out of the pool. He was cold, wet and as close to murdering as he'd ever been in his life. "Thank you," he said, dripping with sarcasm, as well as water. "You can't imagine what a comfort it is knowing you'll no longer wonder whether or not I would have let a drowning woman, even you, die."

"I didn't plan it," Sonny said, backing away as he moved menacingly closer. Seeing his bare chest and arms, every muscle glistening with chlorinated droplets thanks to her, she realized she had seriously underestimated the strength she already considered impressive. "Honest!"

"That's a howl, coming from you."

"The tile was wet and my shoes have slick soles. I slipped!" She shoved a chair in front of him, but he swatted it aside as though it were lighter than Lotti's dinner. "And...and since I was there, I thought I might as well make the most of the situation."

"And faking imminent death comes so naturally to you."

"No!" She glanced behind her, searching for an exit, but found only a maze of pool furniture. "I didn't fake the accident on the mountain, I swear."

"You swear on what? That great repository of truth, *Celebrity* magazine?" He kept advancing.

Sonny stuck out her arm. "Don't come any closer." Her smile felt as damp as it must have looked. "Come on, Trace. I was just yanking your chain, the way I did with the Barrow twins, remember?"

He stalked nearer. "How could I forget? All of Palm Beach knows about the Barrow twins by now!"

"Okay, bad subject," she said. Beginning to really worry about the glint in his eyes, she gave a nervous laugh. "Hey, you don't really think I was seriously testing to see if you'd let me drown, do you?"

"Oh, but I do. And I don't blame you." He backed her into a chaise. As she sprawled over it, he removed the belt from her robe and tied her wrists together.

"What are you doing?!"

Bending, he scooped her into his arms. "I want you to be so completely sure I wouldn't let you sink to the bottom of the pool like some mobster that I'm going to take your little test one more time."

As he carried her to the pool, Sonny kicked up a fury. She guessed her protest had failed when he held her over the water. "You're mad!"

"You're damn right I'm mad, and—"

"Excuse me."

With Sonny in his arms, Trace turned toward the timid voice that had come from behind them. It belonged to a short slightly built bald man wearing glasses.

"I'm looking for the Baroness Sophia Oleska."

"She's all tied up, pal," Trace said. "Ow!" He turned a brutal gaze on Sonny for the pinch she'd given his arm. "Besides, you're a little late. The party was over hours ago."

"Oh, was it? Dear me," the little man said, biting the tip of his thumb. "You see, I didn't know how long she would be among us, and I have something to give her, a token of esteem from our community. But I suppose I'll have to come back tomorrow."

As he walked away, Sonny's only hope of delaying another dunking went with him. "I'm the Baroness Oleska!"

"Oh?" Perking up, the little man returned. "That *is* good news." As he reached into his jacket and withdrew an envelope, Trace reluctantly set her down.

Scrunching a face at him, Sonny held her bound hands out to the man. "Would you mind? There won't be much point in my accepting your lovely gift if I can't open it."

"Oh, oh, by all means." The man tucked the envelope away and went at the knot Trace had made in her belt.

"Ah," Sonny said, casting a smug glance at Trace, "you have no idea how reassuring it is to know there are still true gentlemen in the world."

After the man untied her wrists, he placed the envelope in her waiting hand and to her surprise took off before she could open it and thank him.

Removing the sheet of paper from the envelope, Sonny stepped inside the loggia, beneath a lantern.

"I wonder what Palm Beach could be giving the baroness," Trace said, walking up to her. "Ivana's unlisted number? A lifetime supply of poison for her pen?"

Sonny looked up from the document she held in her trembling hands. So he'd had his revenge, had he? When would she learn? "You ought to know!" Flinging the paper at him, she ran into the house.

Cringing at the slam of the French door, Trace retrieved the paper at his feet. He didn't have to read far before discovering what had so infuriated Sonny. Apparently his attorneys hadn't received the message he'd left earlier this afternoon. She'd just been served with a summons, *his* summons. Unless he wanted to give her cause to accuse him of more cowardice, he couldn't back away from his suit now, even for the pleasure of never having to see her again.

Or could he? Walking to the cabana for a towel, he pondered an intriguing proposition. If he offered to call off his libel suit, would she give him what he wanted in exchange?

8

As THE SUN WOKE Palm Beach to a pink-grapefruit sky, Sonny tiptoed down the grand staircase with her Luis Vuitton luggage and a determination to leave Casa Carlotta before the Whittingtons were up. The summons only ordered her to appear in court, not live under the same roof with the two-faced double-crossing rat who was suing her.

In the great hall, she set her suitcase down and slowly opened the front door, careful to make as little noise as possible.

"You're not leaving already, Baroness?"

Turning, Sonny came face-to-paintroller with Lotti Whittington. She took a step to her right and saw that the chatelaine of Casa Carlotta was wearing new oatmeal-colored overalls, a polka-dot emerald green shirt and a bandanna to match. "I really have to go," she said, glancing out the door for the taxi she'd called earlier. "Besides, I can see you're busy."

"Perhaps you'd care to join me," Lotti said. "I'm sure I have a pair of overalls to suit you. Let's see, what are you—an autumn?"

"Uh, yes," Sonny stammered, reaching for her luggage and backing out the door. "But some other time, per—"

"Don't let her get away, Lotti!" Trace appeared at the top of the stairs. From Sonny's vantage point, he looked shamelessly well rested, not to mention *GQ* handsome in a lightweight white crewneck and khaki shorts. His legs, she noticed as he descended, were out of *Men's Fitness*. "She's probably making off with the family silver."

"Oh, dear. Perhaps I'd better take that," Lotti said, looking at Sonny's suitcase. "Would you mind holding this, dear?"

"I..." Sonny was so startled she accepted the paintroller without a thought as to whether she minded or not. When Trace reached her, she decided she minded very much.

"I want to talk—" Trace took the roller from Sonny when she thrust it in his face. As she turned to make her escape, he snagged her arm with his free hand. "I want to talk to you." While holding onto Sonny, he then turned to his mother and handed it to her. "Luscious Lilac?"

"Yes, dear. What do you think?"

"An excellent..." Slipping behind Sonny, who was struggling to break free of his hold, Trace wrapped his arms around her, hoisted her back into the hall and booted the front door shut. "An excellent choice, as always, Lotti."

"Let me go!"

Trace clamped his hand over Sonny's mouth as he addressed his mother. "You can go back to work now, darling. I can handle things from here."

"If you say so, dear," his mother answered as she walked away. "But if the baroness is making off with your great-grandmother's silver flatware, let her have it. I've always hated that pattern."

"I'd be happy to let her—" Trace broke off at the kick Sonny delivered to his right shin "—have it." He turned her toward him, holding on to her wrists. "You are the most violent woman I've ever met!"

"And you are the sneakiest, most conniving..." Sonny took a breath. "To lure me down here, then serve me with a summons..."

"*Lure* you? Lure *you?*" Laughing, Trace released her. "I think you're a little confused about who the serpent in the garden is, sweetheart. Besides, I didn't know you were going to be slapped with that summons last night."

"No? When did you think I'd get slapped with it—this morning?"

Trace raked back his hair. "You never quit, do you? Look at me. I, Trace Whittington, had no idea you, Sonny Chapin, were going to be served, period. My father asked me to delay any action while you were staying with us, but my attorneys obviously didn't get my message."

"Then how did that weasly little process server know I was here?"

Trace glanced at her luggage, her expensive pale yellow suit, matching shoes, and bag. Her jewelry. "I see you've been to Worth Avenue."

Rubbing her wrists more for effect than easement of pain, Sonny nodded. "The magazine issued me a credit card in the baroness's name."

"Then I imagine all of Palm Beach knew you were in town before the ink dried on your signature." Seeing her troubled expression, Trace cocked his head and gazed at her. "Something tells me the higher-ups at *Celebrity*—oxymoron though that may be—won't be too happy with you when the bills start rolling in."

"They'll get over it once I hand in the story of how I duped your sister into taking me into the bosom of the family," she said, bluffing. Regardless of her fondest wish—to skewer Trace—she knew she'd be treading on thin legal ice in writing anything that might adversely affect Whittington stock. Her relationship with Cort Rockwell, though innocent on her part, would look bad to a jury. But even without that worry, she knew she couldn't have held Diana up to ridicule as she had before. The woman was truly loving and despite all her past mistakes was finally putting her life—and her husband's—back together.

However, Sonny had no such change of heart toward Arthur, whom she still owed for what he'd done to Chapin Industries. She'd just have to find some other way of paying him back.

"I've been giving that some thought," Trace said, opening the door and stepping outside. "Let's get some fresh air and I'll tell you what I have in mind." He offered her his hand. "Please."

Enticed by the sudden change in his demeanor, she placed her hand in his and felt a warmth that couldn't have come from the sun alone. The same warmth she had felt when Terry had held her close.

"The way I see it..." he said, leading her to an exquisite terraced garden and seating her on a stone bench. He propped his foot on it and, crossing his arms on his knee, gazed down at her. "You won't write that story about how you duped my sweet gullible sister."

"And why not?"

"Because you'd have to expose yourself as a fraud, and I don't think that's something the magazine is eager for its readers to find out about its star reporter. Add my libel suit to the mix and—" he leaned closer "—you're in trouble, Sonny."

As his lips neared, Sonny shut her eyes and inhaled sharply. Instantly, she knew she'd made a mistake. A seduction of scents filled her lungs, exotic fragrances that burst into corals and pinks and turquoises before her mind's eye. And wafting through them, the dusky blue-gray of Terry's scent that night on the mountain when he'd kissed her to within an inch of unconsciousness. "I know I am," she murmured. *Big trouble.* Opening her eyes and seeing not Terry but Trace, she moved farther down the bench. "I should think you'd be pleased."

"Oh, I am, but not for the reasons you're imagining." Trace sat down beside her. "You and I are going to make a deal, something you want for something I want."

Her eyes widening with apprehension, Sonny scooted to the end of the bench. "That depends on what you want."

Trace followed, caging her. "Information."

Sonny blinked uncomprehendingly. *"What?"*

"Look," Trace said, sitting forward and pulling the summons from his pocket. "In exchange for your help, I'll call off the suit. Not only that, I'll give you the exclusive rights to one of the hottest financial stories of the year."

Sonny looked askance at him. "What story?"

"Not *what* story," he said. "*My* story. The story of how I took control of Whittington Enterprises, Inc."

Sonny sputtered laughter. "Thanks, but I don't write for the funnies."

Trace shot to his feet. "I'm going after Arthur with or without your help! So take your choice. You can either go along with me now or see me in court later."

Slowly, Sonny rose. "I could almost believe you're serious about this."

"Believe it."

"Why now? Why after all these years?"

Because I looked into the eyes of a woman named Sonny and found my soul. And even if she was a lie, he thought, she'd made him see the truth about himself. "Look, I checked out your story about Chapin Industries last night, and I know you have good reason to want Arthur taken down for what he did to the company. I'm giving you the chance to help me do it. What more do you need to know?"

Sonny couldn't help staring at him, because she couldn't find any signs of either man she had known. None of Trace's pampered blithe arrogance. None of the hesitance she had detected in Terry, for all her loving him. This man's expression bore the stamp of determination; his carriage, a sense of mission. She felt as though she were seeing him for the first time, and she was skeptical. "But I don't see how I can help."

"There's a shareholders' meeting in six weeks," he replied, taking her by the shoulders, urging her to sit back down. "The only chance I have of stopping the renewal of Arthur's contract is to obtain enough proxies from the shareholders to vote it down. And to do that, I need to collect concrete evidence of his mismanagement of Whittington holdings. Not just figures on a balance sheet, but something the average shareholder can understand. That's where you come in.''

"Chapin Industries,'' Sonny said.

"For starters. Is there anybody left there you can trust, people who worked for your father and would still be loyal to him?''

"I think so.''

"Good.'' Taking her arm, Trace rose and steered her through the garden. "Now what about your informant?''

Sonny came to a halt. "You know about Madame X?''

"Is that what she calls herself? Or should I say *he?*''

"Definitely he,'' Sonny replied. She told him about her suspicion that Cort was Madame X and had been using her to drive down the price of Whittington stock in preparation for his takeover.

Throwing back his head, Trace burst into laughter. "My dear Sonny, Cortland Rockwell III can't keep his girlfriends a secret from one another, let alone from his wife. He's incapable of masterminding a hostile corporate takeover.''

That's what you think.

"Besides, the Rockwells divested themselves of Whittington stock last week.''

Sonny looked unconvinced. "Did *he* tell you that?''

"He didn't have to. I heard it from every bartender in town last night. Half of Palm Beach is dumping Whittington stock.''

Sonny sighed. "Then I don't know who Madame X is or how to get in touch with her.''

"Don't worry,'' Trace said, stopping before a camellia bush that was pink with blossoms. "I have a feeling whoever Madame X is, he or she will get in touch with you. So…'' He plucked one lush bloom from the shrub. Turning with it in hand, he searched her eyes, but not for encouragement. That would be asking too much. Just for a hint of cooperation. "What do you say, Sonny? Help me and I'll return this summons to you. You can tear it up, set fire

to it, do anything you want with it. I'll call off the suit.
You have my word." He held the camellia out to her.

Meeting his gaze, Sonny searched for the reason behind
this gesture, which was so uncharacteristically gentlemanly
of Trace Whittington, so confusing to her. But she saw
nothing to explain it other than a sincerity that was new to
her in Trace and even more striking than in Terry. Accepting the flower, she turned away, needing to mull over
his proposition.

But there was nothing to mull over. In exchange for
whatever information she could provide, he was offering to
call off the suit, give her an exclusive on his story—a le-
gitimate news story—and best of all, the chance to stop
Arthur Whittington from gobbling up and destroying other
small companies the way he'd destroyed her father's. How
could she not agree to such terms? On the other hand, if
she did agree to join his battle, for whom would she be
fighting? Trace Whittington, who had given her his word,
a word she couldn't trust? Terry Wright, who had thrilled
her with his kisses and the promise of her sharing in his
unwritten story? He didn't exist. Or this new man, whose
story she *would* write, but who needed nothing more from
her than technical support?

Waiting for her answer, Trace told himself there was still
time to change his mind, time to take back his offer. If she
accepted, they'd be inseparable for the next six weeks. He
didn't know if he could stand it, being near her night and
day, wanting desperately for her to be that other Sonny,
knowing she never could. He'd have to forget her and even
the beautiful baroness he'd danced with last night, and learn
to think of this new Sonny merely as a collaborator. Because without her, he didn't stand a chance of toppling
Arthur six weeks from now.

Slowly Sonny turned back toward him. "Six weeks and
not a minute longer?"

"Not a second longer."

Hesitantly she held out her hand. Trace reached out, and

as his fingers grazed her palm, she commanded her skin to ignore their subtle strength, their warmth. She never found out if her skin would have obeyed because the blare of a horn interrupted their handshake.

Seeing the taxi, Trace told Sonny to ask the driver to wait.

"Why?" she called as he raced across the lawn toward the front door.

"Because I have to throw a few things into a bag. You and I are flying to Chicago!"

Watching him dash in through the entrance to Casa Carlotta, Sonny raised the camellia to her lips. She impressed its delicate texture and sweet fragrance on her memory. "Oh, Sonny," she murmured. "First the mountain. Now the storm."

THUNDER RUMBLED. From behind the wheel of the car she and Trace had rented at Chicago's O'Hare Airport and driven to the parking lot behind Chapin Industries, Sonny studied him. His gaze was fixed so intently on the delivery door at the rear of the building she didn't think he was even aware of her presence. "Are you sure we should be doing this?"

"I wouldn't be doing it if I wasn't sure." Trace looked at his watch. He'd been sitting there for forty-five minutes, trying to ignore Sonny's sweet scent and the two additional freckles on her pert profile, compliments of the South Florida sun. Millie Erwin had better hurry. "Are you sure your contact will come through?"

"My *contact?*" Sonny turned to him. "Trace, that's exactly what's worrying me. You make us sound like spies."

On the other hand, freckles or not, Trace thought, the woman could be vexing. "Look," he said, meeting her anxious gaze, "Whittington, Inc. owns Chapin Industries, right?"

"You don't need to remind me," Sonny replied, turning her face away. But then she felt the warmth of his fingers on her left cheek, and in the next moment, she was looking into his arresting eyes. She found herself wishing she was the object of their intensity, but she knew better.

"Then neither should I need to remind you that I'm a Whittington."

Actually maybe you should, Sonny thought. Bulletins on the hour and half hour so she couldn't possibly forget that the man to whom she was increasingly drawn was the same man who was holding a libel suit over her head. "Okay, I take your point. You have a stake in Chapin."

He had a stake in Chapin all right, Trace thought. Sonny Chapin. *This* Sonny, whose soft, delicate cheek was enticing his fingers to explore her lips and the curve of her throat and… And then they'd get burned on that torch of contempt the real Sonny carried for all things Whittington, especially him. Withdrawing his hand, he faced forward. "So how could I be charged with spying on my own company?"

Folding her arms, Sonny peered at the delivery door through big drops of rain plopping on the windshield. "If we're not spying, why don't we just walk in there and examine everything right out in the open? Why are we waiting for Dad's former secretary to sneak us inside after hours?"

"So Arthur's lackeys won't tip him off that I've been nosing around," Trace replied. "Once he suspects what I'm up to, I won't be able to get into a Whittington subsidiary to examine so much as the bathrooms." Leaning forward, he wiped a circle on the rapidly fogging glass. "Is that Millie?"

Sonny looked at the sturdy, fifty-something woman who had been her father's administrative assistant for more than twenty years. Millie Erwin, he used to say, could run the place as well as he, if not better. Now she stood outside the delivery door, tying a scarf beneath her chin before stepping back inside. "That's the signal. Let's go."

Dashing into the building just ahead of a downpour, Sonny found herself wrapped in Millie's capable arms. She felt as though she was being welcomed home, but she only had to glance around the plant floor to realize that the business that had once dominated its industry wasn't even in the running now.

"It's a disgrace what those number crunchers who take their marching orders from Arthur Whittington have done, Sonny," Millie said. "They've downsized the life right out of this company. My heart breaks every day I come to work and see Edward Chapin's good name on the front door. It's a sacrilege."

"That's why Sonny brought me here, Millie," Trace said, placing a comforting arm around the woman's shoulder. "I want to make Chapin Industries worthy of its founder's name again."

As he walked Millie to the door, Sonny looked on, intrigued. She hadn't realized he was so tall, or maybe he just looked taller next to Millie, though she didn't see why that should be. She'd seen him standing beside his mother, and Millie was certainly taller than Lotti. Then she recalled her conversation with A.W. If the way things appear depends on where you're standing, then maybe she was standing in a new place.

"I want to bring Chapin and other companies like it back to life," he was saying to the woman. Sonny had known Millie since she was a young child, when she used to "work" for her and get paid a dollar an hour for undoubtedly making her job harder. Millie loved the company and Edward Chapin almost as much as Sonny herself did, and evidently Trace sensed that. "Millie, I want to make this company not just profitable but prosperous again, so it can compete and grow and create new jobs. So loyal employees like you can feel proud to work here, and appreciated, the way you did when Mr. Chapin ran things."

Cocking her head at Trace, Millie gave Sonny a puzzled look. "I thought you told me he was a Whittington."

Her gaze meeting his, Sonny smiled. Her perspective *had*

changed, but only because he really was a bigger man than she'd thought. "I did. But now I'm not so sure."

That couldn't be admiration he was seeing in her eyes, Trace thought. Could it? No, it was probably just a general kind of gratitude that somebody was finally attempting to right the wrong Arthur had done Chapin Industries and employees like Millie. Then why did the way she was looking at him make him feel as though he was clad in shining armor and mounted on a white charger? *Get real,* he commanded himself. This place was so filthy the gleam in her eyes was only a reaction to dust. Still, he heard himself say, "Come on, milady. I have dragons to slay and less than six weeks to do it." He took her by the hand. "Show me the operation."

As Sonny guided him around the factory floor, she wondered about his curiously medieval language. Was it possible he, Trace Whittington, the jettingest of the jet set was really beginning to see himself as a warrior knight, a dragon slayer? Funny, but that was what her father had always called his toughest battles—his dragons. And his pet name for her mother had been "Lady Chapin."

Yes, and hers had been Calamity Jane—she was that different from her graceful, gracious mother. When Trace had called her milady, he was, of course, taking aim at the baroness. More and more, she wished she could strangle that odious woman.

"Sonny?" Trace was looking over a row of machinery lining one wall. "What are these?"

"They're crimp machines," she said, joining him. "They stamp the little pins on the ends of the wires inside computer cables, for example."

"What's wrong?" he asked, his forehead wrinkling.

Sonny had felt a shiver at the sight of the machines, but she had thought it so subtle she was surprised Trace had detected it.

Taking a deep breath, she looked away. "I once caught my hand in a machine just like that one." She glanced up at Trace. "Dad was furious with me. He had given me strict orders to stay away from the equipment."

"I can't imagine why," Trace said, smiling.

"Well, there was certainly *that*, my general klutziness," she said. "But there was more to the accident." She explained that against her father's express orders, she and some of the other workers had removed the safety guards from the machines to speed up productivity. Sonny had done it in this one instance because she wanted to help her father meet a deadline to fill an order for his biggest customer. But the others had been doing it routinely to earn bonuses based on output. When her father discovered the practice, the guilty parties expected him to fire them. Instead, he put them on a team of line workers, supervisors and managers that eventually devised a new assembly process that maintained incentives and good pay, but also ensured safety and even improved productivity. "Dad has a real gift for getting people to work together."

Trace wondered if he could ever be the kind of man whose daughter loved and respected him so much she'd risk her own well-being to come to his aid. He could just imagine how furious Chapin must have been, and how overwhelmed. What an unbelievably stupid thing Sonny had done on his behalf, and how incredibly brave. Just thinking about her doing something like that for his sake made him crazy. He wouldn't know whether to shake her or take her in his arms and hold her close. He'd probably do both. He'd probably never have cause to find out. But that didn't prevent him from telling her what he was thinking. He turned her face to his. "I think Edward Chapin's greatest gift is his daughter."

Sonny blinked several times, but each time she refocused on the face before her, it was still Trace Whittington's. "Excuse me?"

He lifted her right hand. "Is this the one that got hurt?" His voice was so low, so soft, so reverent, it stripped away everything she ever knew about him. Or thought she knew. "Yes. I still have a trace of a scar."

Their gazes locked as they simultaneously recognized her unintended play on his name. One corner of his mouth quirked. "I don't doubt it," he said. Raising her hand to his lips, he kissed it.

"Oh," Sonny said softly, recalling the endearing way her father had kissed this same hand years ago. But Trace's kiss wasn't endearing, it was disarming, and his gaze, captivating. It drew her a step closer. As she felt his other arm encircle her waist, her breath quickened. He let go of her hand and touched her cheek, all the while his expression changing from courtly to blatantly and irresistibly male. "Trace? Before, when you called me—"

"Milady," he said, wrapping his other arm around her shoulder, "that's what you are—one helluva lady."

"Oh," she murmured again, feeling like an idiot. But she couldn't think of anything else to say, at least nothing that wouldn't reveal how magnificent his arms felt around her and how she wished he had meant the "my" as well as the "lady." As he pressed her to him, she flattened her palms against his chest. It was hard, like armor, but warm, and she could feel his heart beating inside it. Slowly her hands glided upward over his strong squared shoulders, around his neck. His lips came closer, closer. So close she could—

Scream. "Ahhh!" Sonny jumped back, bumping into the line bench.

"What is it? What did I do?" What the hell *was* he doing?

Sonny hoisted herself atop the bench. "Something just ran across my feet!"

"A roach?"

"Bigger."

"A mouse?"

Panting, she gulped. "Bigger!"

"Rats!" Grabbing a soldering iron from beside one of

the workstations, Trace stalked the area, hunched, yanking chairs, searching under benches.

Sonny crossed her legs and folded her arms. "Are you going to kill them or silver-plate them?"

Straightening, Trace propped his hands on his waist. "What would *you* suggest?"

Looking around for something more lethal, Sonny's eyes were caught by the crimp machine. She frowned. "I'd suggest that the four-legged kind aren't the only variety of rats around here. Take a look at this."

She showed him that the safety guard had been removed from the machine. He inspected the entire row. "They've all been removed." He strode back to her, placing his hands on her waist. "My guess is there's a paper trail of internal memos that will show that the order to remove the guards came from the top. If I can find it, I can show intentional violation of the national safety standards. Then I'll want to get into the files—accounts payable, accounts receivable, the financials. Can you show me where they are?"

The fervor Sonny saw in his eyes sparked a fire in her. Placing her hands on his shoulders, she said, "The offices are up front. Let's go."

As Trace lifted her, gazing into her eyes, he marveled that a woman could be so gutsy yet so delicate. She wasn't a klutz at all. She was just full of passions that, until now, she had been funneling into obtaining revenge rather than into making positive changes. Not that he blamed her. What could she have done on her own? No more than he could without her help.

Sonny recalled the way he'd held her on the mountain, her lips level with his, and how she had been suddenly unable to feel her toes. The only thing she couldn't feel now was restraint. Files, accounts, paper trails, she repeated to herself, trying to get a grip on reality. No matter how serious Trace might be about becoming Whittington's next CEO, he was still the man who had kept an oath to "love 'em and leave 'em." In ten countries.

"If you don't put me down," she said, "we'll never get to accounts payable."

Trace reminded himself of what he had come for. The only problem was that what he had come for couldn't compare with what he wanted, what he needed. This woman, this lady. Who wouldn't be here if he hadn't held a lawsuit over her head. He set her on her feet. "Lead the way."

The storm outside had lessened, but as Sonny and Trace worked late into the night—digging through files, inventory logs, expense accounts, payroll accounts—another more virulent wave of rain, thunder and lightning hit. When the lights in the outer office flickered, Sonny's nerves had taken all they could stand for one night. Between the storm and the skullduggery she and Trace were perpetrating, not to mention the way her heart hammered whenever Trace came near, she'd had it. She walked into her dad's former office where Trace was working, to see how much longer he thought he would be.

She still couldn't get over how different the office looked, not just in comparison to the factory, which was a dilapidated mess, but from its appearance in Edward Chapin's day. The furniture was new, contemporary in styling and expensive. An Aubusson rug overlaid new hardwood flooring. Original oils lined the walls. An entertainment center housed a big-screen TV, VCR and high-end stereo components. The bar was new, too, and stocked with labels that didn't need to advertise in the Sunday circulars. The icing, though, was the addition of a gourmet kitchen. Her father had regularly eaten lunch in the employee cafeteria.

At a window-rattling clap of thunder, Sonny jumped.

"Scared?"

She perched on the corner of the new president's desk, where Trace was poring over reports. "I don't mind telling you, this place gives me the creeps."

"I'm not surprised," Trace said, tossing a pencil on the desk and sitting back. "These guys aren't running lean and mean. They're just running mean." Rising, he paced the room, laying out what he had discovered. Wholesale firings with few replacements and bigger workloads for those who survived. Shortcuts. Shoddy products made of cheaper materials and sold at higher prices. He suspected buyers were taking payoffs from vendors. Why else would they tolerate a string of price increases and never seek competitive bids?

Shoving his hands into his pockets, he stood before a painting. "Not only that, they have lousy taste in art. Damn it, Sonny," he said, turning to her. "Multiply what's going on here by a factor of twenty, and it's not hard to understand why Whittington stock is in the tank. And it's my fault."

As Sonny walked up to him, he turned away as though he was ashamed. He wouldn't even look at her when she touched his arm. "But you challenged Arthur once before! There's no shame in trying and failing."

He sighed. "But there is in giving up."

Sonny stepped in front of him. "Is that what you're going to do now—give up?"

Trace glanced down at her. If for no other reason than his desire to make amends to Sonny and her father, he replied, "No." Long after the shareholders' meeting—regardless of the outcome—long after he'd called off his suit and she had walked out of his life for good, he was going to need a life worth living. For that reason he said, "Never."

To Sonny that "never" sounded like a cry to battle, a battle he clearly intended to win or die trying. If she hadn't been standing here before him, feeling the determination, the sheer force of conviction emanating from every pore in his body, she wouldn't have believed that cry had come from Trace Whittington.

In the past, she conceded, she may have misjudged him. For the present, she believed he had changed. What really shook Sonny was that she cared about the future beyond the shareholders' meeting—his and hers. What if Trace's challenge to Arthur's chairmanship turned out to be only an opening skirmish and not the war? According to the deal she had struck with him, whether he became the new CEO of Whittington six weeks from now or not, she would have fulfilled her part of their bargain. She'd be free to walk out of his life with a summons to burn and a story to sell. But not really free at all. If she had been preoccupied with the Whittingtons before, she would worry about one Whittington ever after. Trace. His war was quickly becoming her war, but she might never see it through to victory with him. In only six weeks he'd call off his suit and she'd never see him again, not even in court.

Thunder exploded. Sonny gasped as Trace wrapped her protectively in his arms. But when she looked over her shoulder to see what he was staring so stonily at, she realized the explosion hadn't been thunder. It had been the door.

"Freeze!" A uniformed cop assumed the stance.

Sonny assumed the worst. She might be seeing Trace in court, after all.

9

"As always, being with you is a unique experience," Trace said. Sitting beside Sonny in the back seat of the patrol car taking them to the precinct station, he refused to look at her. If her sweet neck could talk, it would give thanks he was handcuffed. "I've never had my rights read to me before."

"You certainly don't think *I* have," Sonny retorted, giving him an indignant glare.

Trace returned it. "Why didn't you tell me there was a silent alarm hooked up to the police?"

"If I had known, would we be sitting here doing an episode of *Cops*?" Catching stares from the couple in the car next to them, she hunkered lower in the seat. "Besides, it's certainly not my fault that a power surge triggered it."

Trace laughed sardonically. "No, but it can't be coincidence that the city's worst storm of the season, according to the gendarmes here, blew into town the same day you did."

Sonny's eyes narrowed and her mouth puckered at his attitude, which was a lot more sour than it had a right to be. "Excuse me, but aren't you the guy who was so sure he couldn't be arrested for spying on his own company?"

Trace looked away. He hadn't just been sure, he'd been cocky. Of course, he hadn't considered the possibility that if they did get caught, it might be by cops he would bet had graduated from correspondence school. No matter how many times he explained the situation or how slowly, the pair couldn't make the connection between the "Whittington" on Trace's driver's license and the one on the company letterhead, following "Chapin Industries, a subsidiary of." Sighing, he slid her a glance. "Okay, maybe I *was* wrong. I should have figured the last place the Whittington name would get me into would be a Whittington holding."

Sonny's eyes widened on him. "This can't be an apology I'm hearing. I didn't think Trace Whittington did the mea culpa thing."

"I said *maybe*," he shot back.

Sonny grumbled. "And maybe you saw those warning signs on Cara Mountain, too."

Trace quirked a smile. "Maybe."

"I knew it! I just knew—"

"Look, Sonny," Trace said. He touched her arm with his manacled wrists, coaxing her to face him. "Playing gotcha isn't going to keep us out of the slammer. We have to figure out how we're going to beat this rap."

"First he's James Bond, now he's Al Capone," Sonny said, addressing herself. Suddenly her brow furrowed. "What do you mean, *how?* You'll call your lawyers, they'll explain everything, and we'll be out before they can run a check on..." Seeing him shake his head, she mimicked the motion. "Our fingerprints? What am I missing?"

He edged toward her. "In the first place, all my lawyers can do tonight is get us out on bail. But we need to get the charges dropped, and that could take time. Unless you want to add bail-jumping to burglary, we could miss the shareholders' meeting."

"Oh." Sonny's frown deepened. "What's the second place?"

Trace nudged closer still, so close their thighs touched. "The second place is really the first place, which is that, if I call the Whittington attorneys, Arthur will figure out what I'm up to and we'll have gotten busted for nothing."

Maybe not for *nothing*, Sonny thought, staring at his thigh, recalling the sculpted hardness of it, feeling the press of its solid heat. Feeling like a sickie. She was on her way to jail, and was she worrying about the blisters she was going to get breaking rocks? No-o-o. She was fantasizing about his right thigh and his left and the tush that had looked so tight in those khaki shorts and—oh-oh, better skip that—and his swimmer's torso, and maybe jail was the safest place for her, after all. But not for Trace. He couldn't take control of Whittington from Cell Block Three.

"So what do we do?" she asked. "My father won't be able to do any more than your lawyers, and we can't get Millie involved in this."

Trace hadn't intended for their thighs and hips to meet, but now that they had, he couldn't understand why he hadn't introduced them sooner. The way they took to each other, they were obviously destined, like Fred and Ginger, Warren and Annette, Bonnie and Clyde. Oh, God, they were going to jail and Arthur was going to get away with corporate mass murder. "No, we can't ask Millie to say she let us in. She'll lose her job." He exhaled a long sad breath. "Sonny?"

"Yeah?"

"You don't know how sorry I am I got you mixed up in this. In the first place, I blackmailed you."

A real honest-to-goodness "I'm sorry," Sonny thought with amazement as she stared straight ahead and smiled to herself. "And I suppose the second place is really the first place?"

Looking at the taillights of the car ahead, Trace smiled. "Can't fool you, can I." His smile imploded and his eyes narrowed as he looked at her. "This isn't your fight."

Oh yes it is, you idiot, Sonny thought as she returned his gaze. After a moment she faced forward, laid her head back and inclined it toward his. "Trace?"

"Yeah?"

"For what it's worth, you didn't have to blackmail me."

Closing his eyes, Trace laid his own head back and inclined it toward hers until they touched. "Oh."

"SONNY! ARE YOU ALL RIGHT?"

Outside the police station, in the bright light of mid-morning, Sonny stepped into one of Millie Erwin's earth-mother hugs. Looking over the woman's shoulder, she saw Trace. His hair was a mess, his face shadowed, his eyes red. He was gorgeous. "I'm fine, except for a backache," she replied, arching.

Trace couldn't take his eyes off her. With her shirttail hanging out, her hair sprouting atop her head like a feather duster, her eyes half-shut with fatigue, she looked like a household drudge. No, she looked like a young Audrey Hepburn playing a household drudge, impossibly cute and feminine and, somehow, aristocratic. Milady.

"Are you sure you're all right?" he asked, walking up to her.

"Mmm." She executed an arm stretch. "My cellmate gave me the exclusive rights to her story."

Trace was taken aback. "What was she in for?"

"She threatened to kill her stockbroker." Sonny cleared her throat. "It seems that on his recommendation, she sank a small fortune into Whittington stock the day before its price plummeted thirty percent."

Sympathetic and feeling responsible, Trace rubbed the back of his neck. "Arthur's the one who ought to be in jail."

Sonny lifted one corner of her mouth in a half smile. "Maybe you can get a family rate." But Trace wasn't going to jail, nor was she. The desk sergeant said the charges had been dropped. "Oh, Millie," she said, turning a horrified look on her friend. "You told the police you let us in, didn't you?"

"She did," Trace said, taking both women by the arm and walking them to the diner on the corner. "She told them she let you in because you had a bad case of nostalgia."

"What about you?" Sonny asked.

"I told them he had a bad case of you," Millie replied, giving Sonny a wink.

Her eyes popping with embarrassment, Sonny looked ahead, down, to her left. Everywhere but at Trace. "That was certainly quick thinking," she said stiffly.

And it was certainly true, Trace thought. But obviously not a prospect Sonny welcomed. The one thing he hadn't considered was that she probably had any number of men vying for her, any one of whom she would prefer to the man whose family had made a shambles of her father's business. Maybe there was only one man, a man who didn't come loaded with the kind of baggage Trace carried. The kind of luggage that would give any sensible woman cause to mistrust him. God, he had so much misspent time and squandered personal capital to make up for. "Yes, it was quick thinking," he said, opening the door of the diner for the women. "Unfortunately Millie couldn't come up with anything to exonerate herself."

"Oh, Millie, no," Sonny said as the other woman claimed one side of the booth, forcing her to share the other side with Trace. "You got fired."

"Don't you worry about me, miss," Millie said. "I can take care of myself."

Reaching across the table, Sonny took her hands. "But you were so close to retiring," she said. "Where will you get a job now?"

"With me," Trace said as he slid in beside Sonny, the thrill of his leg touching hers more bracing than the coffees he had just ordered. "Right, Millie? Why don't you tell Sonny what you told me."

Millie explained that after she left them last night, she was so excited about Trace's plan to take control of Whittington, Inc. and restore Chapin Industries that she called the other old-timers who had bought Whittington stock at the time of the acquisition. "We all decided to give our proxies to the man who should be running Whittington," she said, gazing at Trace as though he were a nephew of whom she was proud. "Our shares don't amount to much, but they're a start."

"For which I'm eternally indebted," Trace said, exchanging a look of understanding with Millie. He placed his left hand over Sonny's, which was covering Millie's.

Sonny's eyes slanted at Trace. "I feel like we're the Three Musketeers. What's going on? What did you mean Millie is going to work for you?"

Trace slid his right arm around Sonny. "She's going to help me solicit proxies from the shareholders. Write letters, make phone calls—"

"Twist arms," Millie said.

"And you and I are going retail," he added, turning to Sonny. Without thinking, he drew her hand toward him across the table, joined their palms and meshed his fingers with hers. "We're going to travel the country visiting as many of the shareholders as we can. You'll be there when I make my pitch, when I win and when I lose. How's that for a story?"

Sonny gazed at their hands, at how well they fit, and she felt the strength of his hold on her body, her emotions, her imagination. She could write his story with conviction, with passion. But every story had to end, and when it came to "The Trace Whittington and Sonny Chapin Story," that was the one thing she didn't think she could ever write. The ending. Still, did she really have a choice? With Trace and women, there was always an ending. "It's a helluva story," she said. *Living hell.* "And if there's any justice at all in this world, it will have a happy ending. You'll ride into the sunset as the head of Whittington Enterprises."

Gazing into her eyes, Trace saw maybe not total faith and trust, but support and encouragement. They would do for now. They would have to. But with luck, the others would come. And maybe someday she'd feel the same love and respect he'd discovered he had for her.

SIX WEEKS OF LIVING out of a suitcase, even a Louis Vuitton suitcase, was not something she'd ordinarily care to repeat, Sonny thought. Yet, as she folded and packed the baroness's now well-worn wardrobe, her heart ached, because this was the end of the road. Except for the outcome of the shareholders' meeting ten hours from now, it was the end of the story Trace had given to her exclusively. And what a story it was, the most timeless of all tales— redemption. Of course, the sin usually preceded the redemption, but before they had even left Chicago, Trace set the reverse in motion.

"Candy? Is it really you, darlin'? You'll never guess who this is," he had crooned into the phone while she and Millie, standing in Millie's den, looked on. "Why sweet cakes, I can't believe you remember me after all these years."

The executive secretary at Whittington headquarters in New York not only remembered him, she took him on a nauseating stroll down memory lane. After several minutes of reminiscences that consisted primarily of salacious noises, he murmured, "I think I may be needing a sugar fix."

"I think I may be sick," Sonny said, and stepped into the hall. She heard him say, "Bye, Southern Comfort," and was rolling her eyes when he appeared. "Forgive me for not staying for the—you'll pardon the pun, as my father would say—climax of that little scene. I was afraid of getting socially transmitted diabetes." She propped herself against the wall, crossing her arms and ankles. "Candy, I take it, is an old flame?"

"More like an old heartburn," Trace said. "But she came through."

"Don't you mean across?"

"I mean," he said, backing her to the wall and caging her, "she's faxing a copy of the list of stockholders to Millie's fax machine as we speak."

Sonny focused on his nearing lips. "You're incorrigible."

His mouth brushed hers. "You're wrong."

"You're both on a plane to L.A. in an hour," Millie said, entering from the kitchen. "I just booked your seats." She stared at them staring at her. "Move!"

They'd moved, all right. From cities to plains, in jets and commuter props, in rented cars. In buses and cabs. On foot and in battered old trucks that picked them up on rural roads and deposited them on the doorsteps of the widows of farmers. Sometimes the widows—after Trace had won their proxies with his sincerity and conviction, and the promise to restore the value of their investment—invited them to stay to a fresh-vegetable-and-homemade-bread kind of meal. But mostly they ate in places that served food that would have been indigestible even if they hadn't been in a hurry, places that all seemed to have been decorated by the same clinically depressed interior designer. As they gulped and chewed, they tallied the count of shares they had collected proxies for, crossed names off lists, and charted out their next stops on local maps. And at night they would fall exhausted onto beds in separate rooms in mostly cheap chain motels. The room in Omaha was like the room in Louisville, which was like the one in Montgomery. More than once, when Sonny awoke, she couldn't remember what town she was in. Somehow her geographical disorientation wasn't as frightening as it might have been. All she needed to know was that wherever she was, Trace was next door.

With the exception of her father, Sonny had never seen a man work harder, not just for what he wanted, but for what he believed to be right. He would sometimes spend hours with shareholders, listening, answering their questions, always looking them in the eye and making them believe that their concerns were his concerns. He made her believe, not just once, but every time he met with a shareholder. Often he would leave a shareholder's home or office or mom-and-pop store completely drained, then push on to the next meeting and the next, giving the last person he met that day the same attention he gave the first. Making the same impassioned plea for the last shareholder's proxy as he had made for the first.

All the while Sonny took notes. "Are you getting this down, Ms. Chapin?" he would ask when a shareholder raised a question he needed to look into or made a suggestion for how the company could better market its products. But when she wasn't doing that, she was writing down her observations about the people who owned stock in the company, some of whom were receptive to him, some suspicious, some angry enough to slam the door in his face. He never wavered, never lost courage, never conceded he would do anything but prevail in the end.

At least not in front of her. But often at night she could hear the TV in his room, the volume low, as if to relieve his aloneness. Several times, he went out late and returned in the early-morning hours. From the steadily deteriorating condition of his shoes, she guessed he must have left enough Italian leather on Main Street America to rival D.C.'s Gucci Gulch. It was strange seeing a Whittington literally down at the heels, and somehow endearing. Many times she wanted to take the place of his television or walk beside him on his midnight rounds. But he never asked and she never volunteered. She sensed that although they were, in a sense, partners, there were some things he had to work out for himself.

Unfortunately one of them obviously wasn't his feelings toward her. He remained always polite, even solicitous, making sure she was comfortable or had enough to eat. Asking whether she thought she could visit one more shareholder. Usually she was uncomfortable, famished, and so tired she could crumple. But she never told him so. As long as he could go on, she would go on. She had to go on. Why, she didn't know. Although she bought into his struggle, which she had long recognized was as much for his own soul as it was for that of the company, he clearly had no such investment in her. At least not any longer. She used to think that whether they were Terry and Sonny on the mountain, Trace and the baroness in Palm Beach or a businesswoman and a journalist on a mission, they had, without doubt, shared a powerful attraction.

But in the past six weeks, in the hundreds of hours they'd been practically fused at the hip, he never once tried to kiss her. He never so much as held her hand. And although he always asked for adjoining rooms, he never crossed her threshold, except for the night he had carried her in from the car. Sadly she'd been so dead to the world she had no memory of having been cradled in his arms. When she thanked him the next morning, he said, "No problem," as though what he had done was merely part of his job to bring in the luggage. She knew then that what she had suspected was true. From the moment they left Chicago, he had consciously and deliberately erected a barrier between them. A barrier telling her that, to him, she was a woman whose journalistic services he had negotiated, nothing more. Whenever she was tempted to brush the hair back from his sleeping eyes as she drove, or massage neck and shoulder muscles sore from his own long stint behind the wheel, she reminded herself of the reason she could never be anything more. He might one day forgive, but he could never forget that she had been the Baroness Oleska.

As she folded the dress she had worn that night in Palm Beach, when his jacket button and her lace had entwined, she needed to remind herself one last time. Because six hours from now, when she flew with him to Whittington headquarters in New York, she would be accompanying a man with a long-denied sweet tooth to the Candy store.

TRACE STOOD over the bed in his room tossing socks into his bag. He threw in a tie, pitching it harder than he had the socks, and by the time he'd finished packing, he was hurling fastballs. "Damn it to hell," he said, rubbing the spots of pain over his eyes. For the past six weeks, he'd been living for just one day. Tomorrow. But now that it was only a wake-up away, he felt like he was dying. That was how it felt to realize that after tomorrow, he would no longer be spending eighteen or twenty of every twenty-four hours with Sonny. No more watching for her in motel coffee shops, waiting for her to start his day with the glow of her skin and the smell of her soap and her toothpaste. No more seeing through her bright-eyed and bushy-tailed act. He knew she couldn't have averaged more than five hours' sleep a night. He didn't flatter himself her act was for his benefit. She was Edward Chapin's daughter, all right, strictly a never-complain, roll-up-the-shirtsleeves-and-get-to-work kind of woman. He'd lost track of the number of times her suggestion they drive another hundred miles or catch one more hop before calling it a day had renewed his spirit and given him the strength to press on.

There was only one time, halfway through their cross-country trek, when that extra hundred miles had been too much, even for her. It was about two in the morning and she had been asleep beside him for the past hour when he finally found a place to stay—one of those 1950s motor courts that would have grown up to become a Ramada Inn if the interstate had gone in there, instead of two miles east. After he'd checked in and driven to their rooms, he'd tried rousing her, gently at first.

"You're doing a great imitation of Arthur's late wife, Sonny," he said after she had failed to respond to his—by now—not-so-gentle nudges. "But how about doing it inside? I have a feeling if we don't get back on the road before daylight hits this place, we're going to find out we just spent the night in the Bates Motel. Sonny?" He patted her cheek, but her head only slumped onto her shoulder. "Sonny!"

As he had run to the other side of the car, he'd prayed. For the first time since he was a child, he'd prayed so hard it hurt. "Please, God, let her be all right. I'll take longer walks, colder showers, I swear. Just let her be all right."

When he opened her car door and saw her inhale a breath

of chill air, he gave thanks. She wasn't dead, just dead tired. After he unlocked her room and turned down the sheets, he carried her inside—holding her very close and very dear—and laid her on the bed. Tucking her in, he'd leaned over her sweet face and kissed her once, slowly, on her lovely mouth. If he was going to take another, colder shower, he might as well indulge the need for it.

Sleeping next to her these past weeks with nothing more than a thin wall separating them had been torture. She was, he had learned, a political junkie, and he loved listening to her debate, often in colorful terms, her journalistic colleagues on C-SPAN. He would picture her adorable outrage at what she considered to be idiocy, see her pacing the floor—barefoot—gesturing at the TV, that oversize flannel shirt she had picked up in Tacoma riding up her bare thighs. Then he would have to take a shower. And when he returned to bed and switched off the light, he could hear the drawers of her dresser sliding open and closed, and imagine her unbuttoning her shirt. He could see her reaching around her back and unhooking her bra, then slipping out of her panties and into a silk teddy. Then he would have to go for a walk. Thank God, it wasn't winter or he'd have caught pneumonia weeks ago.

But he had seen the disdain in her eyes in Chicago, after he had sacrificed for the cause and sweet-talked the list of shareholders out of Candy. "Incorrigible," she had called him. Given what she knew about a reputation he hadn't cared enough to restore—until now—he hadn't blamed her. He had vowed then and there to prove to her that he *had* changed. He wanted her to witness that he respected women in general and revered her in particular, and that he could virtually live with her night and day without once making a pass or so much as a suggestive remark. Unfortunately his loving her from afar hadn't brought her nearer to trusting him. She had maintained a spatial relationship to him that was so constant—so constantly distant—he was beginning to think it was an immutable law of physics.

Apparently she had no intention of breaking it tonight, either. They were spending their last night together as they had spent all the past nights—alone in their rooms.

Staring at the wall between them, Trace made up his mind. He crossed to his dresser and pulled out the two things he'd been saving for this night—Sonny's summons and a bottle of warm champagne he'd been carrying around since L.A. "You," he said, pointing to the wall, "are coming down."

THE LAST THING Sonny had packed was the bottle of champagne, the kind left over from New Year's Eve parties where Tex Mex dip is served. Millie had stowed it in her suitcase with a note that said, "For a special occasion." Maybe tonight wasn't special, Sonny thought, but it was the last occasion she would have to tell Trace what these six weeks had meant to her, how much she admired his dedication, and to wish him well. Taking the bottle from her bag, she walked to her door, which faced the parking lot, and stepped outside. As she turned toward Trace's room, she gasped, clutching the champagne to her.

"Great minds," Trace said, smiling and showing her the bottle he carried.

"Judging from the labels, your mind runs to France and Millie's to the corner drugstore," Sonny replied. They laughed, then turning, Trace walked to his door and Sonny to hers. They unlocked them and entered their rooms. After a moment they each leaned through their doorways, looking for each other.

"Don't say it," Sonny said.

"I wouldn't think of it."

Then together, "Your place or mine?"

Trace tossed a coin and won, taking the bottle Sonny handed him. "Do you really think we'll need this?"

"You never know," she shot back. "We might run out of gas on the way to the airport tomorrow."

They laughed again, then Trace said, "That was sweet of Millie. I think we ought to drink a toast to her."

"Something like, 'One for all and all for one'?"

"Yes," Trace said, his voice suddenly dropping to a smoky depth as he peered into her eyes. "All for one." *Milady.*

One what? Georgia Peach? Sonny moved to a chair near the window, beside the table where he'd been tallying the number of shares the proxies he'd collected represented. "Where do we stand, Trace?"

Suddenly his heart no longer felt like a concrete block. They'd been all over the country, and now, finally, they were getting somewhere. "I know exactly where *I* stand, Sonny, but—"

"What I meant," she said, not wanting to hear what she already knew about his appetite for Southern cooking, "is where are we on proxies? With what Millie's collected, do we have enough shares to outvote Arthur tomorrow?"

Trace felt the hope leave his heart. She had mixed signals again, but this time, the joke was on him. Setting the champagne on the table, he sat opposite Sonny, picked up the stack of papers and fanned it. "It's too close to call," he said. "Too many variables. We've had a lot of pledges, but any proxies Millie doesn't receive before she leaves for New York tomorrow will automatically be voted for Arthur. Of course with my luck," he said, recalling another last night, in Monte Carlo, "she'll get stuck in a holding pattern over Kennedy, and—"

"Don't say that!" Sonny leapt to her feet. "This has nothing to do with luck, Trace." She sat on her heels before him and laid her hands over his. "You're infinitely smarter than Arthur. You have more vision, more courage..." She rose, looking down at him. "One thing the baroness wrote I'll never apologize for was that you're the Whittington son who deserves to inherit the chairmanship of the company."

Slowly Trace, too, got to his feet. He didn't give a damn what the baroness thought. Placing his hands around her upper arms, he drew her close. "Is that what Sonny Chapin is going to write?"

His touch was searing and his lips so near she could feel their heat. Sonny felt woozy and wanted him to both let her go and never let her go. "I'm going to write the truth," she said, breathless. "You have nothing to worry about."

Easy for you to say, Trace thought. To Sonny he was just a story, a way to step up from tabloid journalism. But how was he going to convince her that there would never have been a story for her to write if she hadn't fallen into his arms that morning on the mountain? Maybe if he wiped out past debts, they could start over. "That reminds me," he said, releasing her and reaching into his shirt pocket. "In a few hours all hell's going to break loose, so I'd better give this to you now."

Sonny recognized the court summons he had promised she could destroy at the end of their journey. Instead, taking it back would destroy her. After tomorrow she'd never see him again. Without looking at it, she stuffed it into her jeans pocket. "Well," she said, putting on a smile, "I guess that's that. Contract fulfilled. What are we waiting for? Let's celebrate." Turning away as tears welled in her eyes, she moved to the dresser against the wall between their rooms where there were two glasses and a plastic ice bucket on a tray. She picked up the bucket and went to the door. "I think there's an ice machine a few doors down."

"I'll go," Trace said, taking the container from her. A lady didn't fetch ice. Besides, if he didn't cool down his libido, he might put his fist through that damn wall. But when he opened the door, he walked into another wall of sorts. One about six foot four and three hundred pounds. "Something I can do for you?" he asked, wishing he'd narrowed the field of possible answers.

The Wall forced Trace back into the room with Sonny, and he locked the door behind him. "Yeah," he said, looking around. "You got any cards?"

Trace and Sonny looked at each other, then at The Wall. "Cards?"

"Yeah," the Wall said, squeezing into one of the chairs. "It's going to be a long night."

Sonny grabbed Trace's arm as he shoved her behind him. "You sure you have the right room?" he asked.

The Wall removed his sunglasses. "You sure you're Trace Whittington?"

Sonny felt Trace's spine steel. "Who wants to know?"

Grinning, The Wall twiddled his thumbs over his sumo wrestler's belly. "Somebody who'd like you to stay put until ten o'clock tomorrow morning."

The time set for the shareholders' meeting. Sonny and Trace exchanged a glance, then spoke simultaneously.

"Arthur."

10

SONNY SAT RIGIDLY on the arm of Trace's chair watching him deliberately lose at gin rummy as he plied their keeper with Millie's cheap champagne. Obviously he thought his only hope of overcoming Arthur's hired muscle was to slow the man's reflexes and at just the right moment take him off guard. But so far, the only thing that was slowing was the rate of the man's drinking. She checked the time. Their plane left for New York in less than two hours. She had to *do* something. Now.

Leaving Trace, she sat on the bed opposite The Muscle. Unbuttoning her shirt, she bared one shoulder, crossed her legs and struck a sexy pose. He didn't notice. She cleared her throat, and when both men glanced at her, she puckered her lips and batted her eyes at The Muscle, giving him a come-hither look.

"You have something in your eye, Sonny?" Trace said, grinning.

"Nah, she's trying to distract me," The Muscle said. "Nice try, lady, but I'm a married man. Gin."

Sonny straightened her shirt and saw Trace struggling not to smile. Incensed, she shot to her feet. "I suppose Candy could have succeeded where I failed!"

Unable to contain himself any longer, Trace let out a chuckle. "No doubt," he said. But then he sobered and looked deeply into her eyes, desperate for her to know—despite her not returning his feelings—how much he loved her. "But, Sonny, it wouldn't make me crazy if she had."

What was that supposed to mean? "Are you saying it wouldn't bother you that a woman, any woman, would turn herself into bait for this Neanderthal?"

"Hey!" The Muscle drained his glass.

"Of course it would bother me," Trace shot back at her. Couldn't she see he was only trying to tell her that if the guy had laid a finger on *her,* he would have gone berserk. "But that's not what I meant. I *meant*—"

"How about crackin' that other bottle?"

Now he wants another drink, Trace thought, reaching for the imported champagne. Suddenly, it occurred to him that if he could shake it without The Wall noticing, then aim the cork at his eye—

"I'll take that," The Wall said, grabbing the bottle. After popping the cork single-handed, he guzzled the overflow, then started to pour.

"Wait," Trace said, putting his hand over the top of The Wall's glass. "You obviously have a discerning palate, my friend." Turning to Sonny, he handed her both glasses and asked her to rinse them free of the polluting residue of the cheaper wine. "And be careful, dearest. You know how clumsy you are. I wouldn't want you to hurt yourself...or anyone else."

Sonny felt the burn rise to her cheeks. How dare he treat her like an errand girl, then condescend to her, and in front of this oaf? As she started a comeback, he gave her a look that stole her words. "Go on, my little hot potato. And be careful on your way back."

Little hot—? Yech! What had gotten into him? He knew she detested such drivel. Puzzled, Sonny went into the bathroom. Lifting the faucet control, she stuck one of the glasses beneath the stream, then snatched it back with a curse. Damn, the water was hot. Her gaze flew to her astonished reflection in the mirror. Hot? It was scalding! A moment later she took a deep breath and started back, a glass in each hand held near the rim. As she passed the foot of the bed, she telegraphed a glance to Trace. Receiving it, he gave her a barely perceptible nod.

Taking the cue, she tripped, lunged forward and dumped two full glasses of scorching water on The Muscle's head. Palming his face and bellowing, he tried to get up. But before he could heave his bulk out of the chair, Trace smashed the bottle on his head. Like a felled tree, the man crashed facedown on the table.

Sonny quickly took his pulse, then, satisfied he was only unconscious, shrugged. "Well, he did ask us to crack the bottle." When she turned toward Trace, he took her in his arms and kissed her hard, so hard her knees turned soft.

"Madam, you are poetry in motion!"

"Yeah," she said, recovering her balance and helping him gather the proxies. "But I never got my Dom Perignon."

"Look at it this way," he replied, hurrying her out the door. "You'll bag Arthur Whittington's head over your word processor, instead."

"Terrific," she said, returning to lay the Do Not Disturb sign on The Muscle's back. *Now if I could just win Trace Whittington's heart for the rest of my life.*

AFTER TRACE AND SONNY hit the Kennedy tarmac, New York hit them with every conceivable delay, including a reroute around a demonstration outside the U.N. Realizing they weren't going to have time to freshen up and change at her apartment before the meeting, they directed the cabby to the Whittington Building. But they still had to get out and run the last three blocks to have any hope of preventing the vote to renew Arthur's contract. At ten-twelve, after the elevator had already stopped at every floor, they spilled out and climbed the remaining six flights to the conference room where the meeting was in progress. As they approached the walnut double doors, the first thing they noticed was who and what weren't there. Millie and the proxies she had received by mail.

"Maybe she's gone inside," Sonny said, trying to catch her breath.

Trace cracked the door, eyed the security guard, then scanned the sparse audience. "Or maybe she's just gone."

"She could be stuck in traffic." Please God, Sonny prayed, just don't let it be a holding pattern. They'd come too far to be defeated by a cluster of blips on a radar screen.

Trace scoped out the dais, where Arthur sat surrounded by A.W., Diana and the other directors. The treasurer stood at the podium, droning the year-end statement. He turned to Sonny. "It's okay, they haven't voted yet. But I'll have to stall them."

He took her by the hand, but she held back. "Trace? Whatever happens in there, it doesn't matter. I already have the ending to my story." Rising on her toes, she kissed his cheek. "Now, go slay your dragon, Galahad."

Overwhelmed, Trace barely managed to swallow the lump in his throat, let alone say what was in his heart. On the mountain he had brazenly suggested she call him Galahad because he'd rescued her, sort of. Actually he hadn't deserved knighthood then, and he wouldn't deserve it now, except for her. He was about to take the biggest gamble of his life, stake his entire fortune against Arthur's chairmanship. No, that wasn't the real risk. He was wagering his soul against his pride, rolling dice he should have rolled years ago. Thanks to Sonny. These past six weeks she had restored his faith in himself, made him believe not only that he could be the next CEO of Whittington Enterprises, Inc., but that he was destined to be. She had been right a moment ago. Whatever happened in there, he was embarking on a new life, a life he owed to her. A life that would never be complete without her. "Sonny, I—"

"I'm sure we all appreciate the fine presentation made

by our treasurer,'' he heard Arthur say into the microphone. ''Now Mr. Lackey, our secretary, will conduct the voting.''

''Hold it, Lackey!'' Trace burst into the room with Sonny in tow. He flashed his ID at the guard, who bowed to the Whittington name and let them pass despite their present resemblance to a pair of fugitives. ''Relax, folks,'' he said to the shareholders craning their necks at the two of them as they walked up the center aisle. ''I just want to make sure everything goes according to Hoyle.''

Brian Baird, half turning his wheelchair, greeted them with a smile. ''I'm glad somebody does,'' he murmured.

Trace seated Sonny on Brian's right, but remained standing in the aisle, his iron-hard gaze nailing a badly shaken Arthur with a declaration of war. ''You look as though you've seen a ghost, Artie. You know, you really should get out more. But then, that's why I'm here. To see that you get out.''

Arthur's eyes were eerily invisible behind the glare on his glasses, but Trace and Sonny both saw the thin cords straining on either side of his neck. ''If you'd care to take your seat, Mr. Lackey will proceed with the voting,'' he said, seemingly undeterred. He had to know Trace didn't yet control enough stock to carry out his threat. And time was on Arthur's side.

Clutching a fistful of shirt at her stomach, Sonny turned to look at the doors at the back of the room. No sign of Millie. And without Millie, who'd been the headquarters for their proxy-gathering campaign these past weeks, Trace wouldn't have the votes he'd need to take over the company. She looked at Trace. ''What are you going to do?''

''Something I used to do well,'' he said, his voice low. ''Waste time.'' He turned to the dais. ''Mr. Chairman! Have the minutes of the last annual meeting been read?''

Arthur grabbed the neck of the microphone as if to tear it off its stand. ''We dispensed with the reading of the minutes as we have more pressing matters at hand.''

"As a stockholder I have a right to demand the minutes be read," Trace said. He shrugged. "So I'm demanding."

Amidst a few snickers from the audience, Sonny saw Arthur wire to his brother the most malicious sneer she had ever seen. Nevertheless, he had no choice but to direct the secretary to read the minutes.

"That should buy us about ten minutes," Trace said. Sonny watched him give his brother-in-law a firm two-handed handshake, then squat beside him. "Brian, there's something I'd like to clear up about what I said in Palm Beach, about us playing—"

"You know, Trace, I love your sister to death, but she can be a real scatterbrain." Brian broke into a broad grin. "Hell, I didn't even know she *had* a younger brother until the night she introduced you to me."

Sonny's gaze flew to Trace. If she could just get him to look at her, she could tell him with her eyes, and from her heart, that she understood what Brian was saying. That Trace really hadn't known his brother-in-law was partially paralyzed because no one had told him. But with so little time and in such a public place, how could she also tell him she had known as much since the first time she saw him gently reassure a frail elderly shareholder afraid of losing his nest egg that he would do everything in his power to preserve it? For nearly two months she had realized that he was naughty enough to seduce the baroness for spite, but he could never knowingly be cruel.

Oh Trace, she thought, *I should have told you before that I'd misjudged you. I would have, if I hadn't been afraid I wouldn't also blurt out how much I love you.*

Trace couldn't bring himself to look at Sonny. He'd look for all sorts of things in her eyes, in her heart, he knew he wouldn't find. Instead, he focused on Brian, grateful for his brother-in-law's understanding. "Welcome to the family," he said.

Sonny smiled despite Trace's shutting her out, keeping

a professional distance. The newfound affection between the two men, both of whom she had come to admire in different ways, swelled her heart.

Brian glanced at the dais. "Looks to me like you're the one who could use a welcome. Good luck, brother."

Trace looked over his shoulder at the double doors, then at Sonny. "Unless Millie gets here with those proxies soon, it's going to take more than luck."

If Sonny had been worried before, when the secretary finished reading the minutes, she panicked.

Trace took a deep breath. "This is it, Sonny," he said. "I'll take them now."

Reaching into her tote, she withdrew a manila envelope containing the proxies she and Trace had collected. Six weeks' worth. The six most unforgettable weeks of her life. Handing them over was like saying goodbye. No, it *was* saying goodbye. She couldn't bear to look at him, but then, she couldn't bear not to.

Trace stared at the envelope. Each of the proxies it contained represented more than votes. Old Mr. Martin and his retirement income were there, and the Fongs, an immigrant couple just starting out. And Mrs. Dean, who was worried she wouldn't be able to leave as much to her church as she had hoped. But most of all, Sonny was there. Sonny, who had worked as hard as he had to obtain those proxies, given up as much sleep, gotten as much indigestion. Cared as much about what happened to those people and their investments as he did. For a moment, as he took the envelope, he felt he held her heart in his hand. But when he voted those little slips of paper, where would it go? Where would he find it again? Taking the envelope, he gazed into her eyes. "Sonny, where will you—"

"The vote is on the proposal to renew the term of office—"

"Mr. Chairman!" As Trace started toward the dais, he felt Sonny's fingers on the heel of his palm. Without looking back at her, he squeezed them, then hurried on. "Mr. Chairman," he said, climbing the dais. "I'd like to know if a quorum is present. A vote isn't valid without a quorum."

"All right," Brian whispered, pulling a fist.

Sonny cast him a smile, then glanced once again at the doors, only to be disappointed again. With obvious fury at his brother, Arthur had ordered the quorum. While it was taken, Sonny watched Trace shake hands with his father and the other directors, except for Diana. His sister he kissed on the top of her now brunette head as he tenderly brushed her cheek with his palm. Sonny couldn't be sure, but she thought she saw him mouth the words "I love you" as Diana gazed up at him.

With the quorum established, Sonny began gnawing on her knuckles. She knew Trace was running out of procedural-delay tactics. He was going to have to launch his challenge to Arthur's chairmanship without the votes to back him up. The secretary stepped to the microphone to begin the vote.

"Mr. Chairman," Trace said.

Arthur ignored him. "Proceed, Mr. Lackey."

Trace rose from the chair he had taken beside his sister and stood tall. "Mr. Chairman, I submit my name for the position of chairman and chief executive officer of Whittington Enterprises, Inc."

"You can't nominate yourself, Trace," Arthur said, waving him off as if he were a gnat. "It's against the rules."

Sonny held her breath as a hope-crushing silence descended on the room. Neither she nor Brian were shareholders. They couldn't nominate Trace.

Mr. Lackey adjusted the microphone. "The vote is on a proposition—"

"Mr. Chairman." Diana Whittington Baird rose from her seat. "I wish to nominate Trace Whittington for the office of chairman and chief executive officer of Whittington, Inc.''

Sonny, along with the rest of the gathering, turned toward the sound of clapping from the left side of the room. "I second the nomination. You give 'em hell, Trace!"

Gaping with delighted astonishment, Sonny met Trace's glance. The woman on her feet, applauding him, was Mrs. Dean, the church lady, all the way from Boise.

Mr. Lackey looked helplessly at Arthur, awaiting instructions. Arthur clenched his bloodless fists atop the table at which the directors and officers were seated, then with a jerk of his head, ordered the secretary to announce Trace as a write-in candidate.

God bless Mrs. Dean, Sonny thought, but where was Millie?

Mr. Lackey ran his finger under his collar. "The vote is on—"

"Mr. Chairman!"

Sonny turned around, then broke into a huge grin. *Mr. Martin!*

"Mr. Chairman," the old man began, "before we vote, I'd like to hear the candidates speak about how they intend to improve the company and its earnings."

The room suddenly hummed with a buzz of agreement.

Arthur stared at each of the shareholders, measuring their threat to his agenda and appearing to find it minimal. "Oh, very well," he replied, tossing his Montblanc pen on the table and stepping to the microphone. As if he couldn't be more bored, he gave a two-minute speech about how conglomerates worldwide were experiencing depressed markets and rising labor costs. He cited economically obscure ratios of this to that and concluded that, all things considered, Whittington was holding its own very nicely, thank you. In other words, the mess the company was in wasn't his fault.

When Trace stepped to the podium, Sonny touched praying hands to her lips.

"My brother is a knowledgeable man," he began, grasping the sides of the podium and craning a glance at Arthur. "About facts and figures and bottom lines." He focused a spellbinding gaze on the audience. "But he doesn't know squat about people, and that's what businesses are about, from the mom-and-pop grocery to the multinational corporation. People. Engineers and stock boys, managers and shipping clerks, receptionists and data processors, all striving for individual excellence while working toward a common goal. Stockholders investing their savings and their faith in those people and their ideas. At least that's what Whittington would be about if I were the chairman and CEO."

Feeling the sort of chills she got when she heard Pavarotti sing, Sonny hugged herself. Trace was hitting high C. But it was a performance that would go to waste unless—

Trace stopped talking.

Hearing a commotion at the back of the room, Sonny turned around. "Yes!" Millie Erwin stood at the door like a tour guide ushering a steady stream of people into the room. She hadn't just brought the stockholders' proxies, she'd brought the stockholders. Soon every available seat was filled, including the one next to Sonny, which Millie occupied.

"When I told them how wonderful Trace was and how he wanted to revitalize the Whittington companies, they all wanted to come to the meeting," she whispered. "At the last minute, I had to hire two extra buses to collect them all from the airports and train stations and bus depots." The two friends clasped hands as Trace continued his speech.

In the next twenty minutes he went on hitting the right notes, talking about the abuses, mismanagement, outmoded practices, and timidity the current leadership had fostered.

He explained what he would do differently, laying out a vision for the company and its future that, when he had finished, brought the crowd to its feet, cheering.

While Sonny stood, grinning and applauding and thinking this was like one of those moments in a Frank Capra film when underdog Jimmy Stewart wins the day, she detected motion to her left where there should have been none. Turning her head, she watched Brian rise from his chair, stronger, straighter, steadier. Using his thumb and forefinger, he gave a rousing whistle. Exchanging grins with him, she summoned a deep breath and joined in.

But cheers and whistles weren't enough, Sonny thought as she sat down. Trace needed votes, and there was no way of knowing if he had them. Most of the stockholders who had come to support him were small investors. Whether or not they controlled enough shares to outvote the numbers the directors controlled, even if Diana was to vote all her shares for Trace this time, was doubtful. But as Arthur took Trace's place at the podium, the perspiration he was mopping from his waxy brow bolstered Sonny's hopes. He was worried. Very worried.

"Let me say I share my brother's vision for the future," he began, "but it takes more than vision to run a company like Whittington, Inc. It takes training and experience. I'd like to remind the shareholders and especially the board, which shares responsibility for the company..."

"Meaning the directors can be sued for screwing up," Brian said, leaning toward Sonny. "He's telling them what they already know. It's safer to stick with the status quo."

Sonny's hopes crashed like The Muscle after Trace had beaned him with the champagne bottle. In their frenzy to collect proxies, they had forgotten about Arthur's ace in the hole.

"...that for over one hundred years, an Arthur Whittington has been at the helm of Whittington, Inc."

The Arthur Factor! As Sonny shot to the edge of her

seat, she noticed A.W. motion for the guard. Was he anticipating that the battle between his sons would turn physical?

"From the time I was a child, my father, Arthur Whittington IV, prepared me for this awesome responsibility,"
Arthur intoned, "while my brother has followed in the footsteps of his namesake, our uncle, who has never been able
to commit himself to anything but a game of baccarat in
his entire life."

"That's right!" one of the stockholders, whom Sonny
knew was undecided, shouted. "This guy Trace talks a
good talk, but for the past five years, he's been nothing but
a playboy."

"I agree," another undecided, a woman, said. "Have
you read those articles about him in *Celebrity* magazine?"

"Yeah, by that Baroness-What's-Her-Name!"

Cringing, Sonny buried her head in her hand.

A woman with a birdlike voice spoke. "I always say
tradition should be preserved. There isn't enough attention
paid to tradition these days. Whittington, Inc. has always
been run by a firstborn son. Why, I've had my stock since
Arthur Whittington III ran the company."

As the discussion continued to bode ill for Trace, Sonny
felt Brian nudge her. When she looked up, she saw the
guard holding a folded scrap of paper out to her.

"Are you Ms. Chapin?"

Puzzled, she hesitated answering. "Yes," she said at last,
her tone tentative.

"Mr. A.W. says you'll need this."

Even more confounded, Sonny accepted the note and, as
the guard returned to his post, opened it. "Alhena?" she
mouthed, clueless as to the meaning of the word scribbled
on the paper. Then, reading the signature, she looked up at
A.W. through eyes wide with disbelief. *Madame X?* A.W.,
not Cort Rockwell, was the secret informant who'd sup-
plied her with the ammo she'd fired at Arthur in her *Ce-*

lebrity column? But that made no sense. Why would he want to expose Arthur's abuses and jeopardize Whittington stock?

For the same reason, she quickly deduced, he had sent her this note. He had wanted to break Whittington, Inc.'s cycle of dependency on firstborn males named Arthur. He had wanted his younger son to wrest the reins of leadership from his incompetent and corrupt older son, and he had used her column to lure Trace home, prompt him to challenge Arthur. Surely, A.W.—a savy businessman himself— would never have pursued so reckless a scheme unless he had the goods to see it through. If A.W. knew how to overcome objections to Trace's not being his rightful successor, and was unwilling—or unable—to reveal the information himself, that could mean just one thing: he had almost certainly encrypted it in the note she now held in her fingers.

Unfortunately she was nowhere near to breaking the code. "Alhena" meant nothing to her, though it did sound vaguely familiar. She shifted her recall into high gear. *Alhena, Alhena.* Where had she heard that name before? As she frantically searched her memory, she saw a female shareholder—eager to get a closer look at the blood feud erupting on the dais—raise a pair of small binoculars to her eyes.

Of course! That was where she'd heard the term "Alhena"—in A.W.'s observatory in Palm Beach, the night he'd shown her Castor and Pollux through his telescope. Though the stars were twins, Pollux alone had a "mark" on his feet—the smaller star, Alhena.

Great, Sonny thought, crumpling the note. How did A.W. expect Trace to use this bit of astronomy trivia to convince a roomful of irate and risk-averse shareholders to put anyone other than an Arthur Whittington at the helm of Whittington, Inc.?

Clumping a fistful of hair in frustration, she silently grumbled over the sheer idiocy of staking the future of a major corporation and thousands of jobs on something as arbitrary as the order of a man's birth and who he was named for. She wondered if Trace's namesake, A.W's twin brother, had ever cursed the few minutes' difference in their ages, minutes that had permanently relegated him to second-class status. She wondered if he had ever wished he could have traded places with his more fortunate firstborn twin.

Twin. Brother. Trading places. As the words mingled in her mind, Sonny began to glimpse light, starlight. In his observatory that evening A.W. had divulged another bit of trivia—family trivia—along with his astronomy lesson. Like Pollux, the elder Trace Whittington bore a mark on his foot, a scar resulting from a childhood accident. Otherwise, according to A.W., he and his brother were indistinguishable. Had he meant to tell her that they could have switched identities without anyone detecting their ruse—as long as they kept their shoes and socks on? "Alhena," she murmured. "Al—"

"Alhena!" Leaping to her feet, Sonny ran up the aisle.

"Out of order!" Arthur hammered his gavel on the podium. "You'll have to sit—Baroness!" Recovering from his momentary shock, Arthur banged the gavel harder. "You're out of order!"

"No, *you're* out of order," she shouted back, climbing the dais. "Birth order!"

"Guard!" Arthur waved the security guard to the dais as Sonny scooted past the gaping directors toward A.W., only to be stopped by Trace.

He grabbed her by the shoulders. "I don't know what you think you're doing, but..." He saw the guard lumbering toward them with his hand on his holster. "I don't want you getting hurt."

"Let me go, darling, please!" She shrugged out of his hold. "A.W.!" she cried, lurching to the end of the table. "Take—"

The guard grabbed her, but she fought his rough grasp. Trace fought the guard, landing a punch on what apparently was a glass jaw. The man keeled over the edge of the dais as the audience released horrified cries.

"It's all right, everyone," Sonny called out, quelling the stockholders' babble. As they stood watching her in stunned silence, she turned again to A.W. "Take off your shoes, A.W. Your socks, too."

Trace whipped her around. "You *do* have a foot fetish!"

"Oh, for Pete's sake," she said, snatching her arm away. "Trace, think. Do you know of any way to tell your uncle Trace and your father apart?"

"What?"

"*Do* you?"

"No. They're absolutely identical."

"This is preposterous," Arthur said. "Lackey, send for the police."

"Yes do, Lackey," Sonny said, turning on Arthur with ferocity. "I'm sure they'd love to know how Arthur Whittington hired a thug to keep his brother locked away until the voting was over and he was reelected chairman and CEO."

Arthur gave her a murderous glare, but held Lackey in place.

Sonny turned to Diana. "Quickly, Dee, quickly, do *you* know any way of telling your uncle and your father apart?"

"No, I— Wait." She looked at A.W., who was untying his shoes. "I remember when I was staying with my grandparents one summer, they gave me a bicycle. My grandfather Whittington told me to be sure to wear sturdy shoes because Uncle Trace had cut his foot badly on his own bike when he was a child."

"I never knew that," Arthur and Trace said in unison, then scowled at each other.

Diana beamed, quite proud of herself. Sonny gave thanks that if there could only be one thing Diana remembered, it had been that. "A.W.," she said, walking up to him. "Show us your feet."

"I see what you're trying to prove," Arthur said, breaking through the throng gathered around A.W. "But it won't work. My father recently stepped on broken glass and took stitches. So of course, he has a scar on his foot."

"A.W.?" Sonny gazed into his expressionless eyes. If she was wrong, she'd not only have made a complete fool of herself, she'd have done Trace more harm than good.

A.W. stared back at her, then pushing away from the table, lifted one bare foot onto it. A pink line zigzagged across the ball of it.

"You see?" Arthur pointed at his father's sole. "That's obviously a fresh scar."

All eyes turned to Sonny, who turned to A.W. She took a deep breath, "Alhena," she said, commanding him to reveal his other foot.

Slowly A.W. lifted it onto the table. Crouching down, Sonny, Trace and Arthur examined it. Two thin faint white lines intersected across the heel, forming a perfect—

"So that's where you got the idea to call yourself Madame X," Sonny said, breaking into a grin.

"You?" Trace gaped at his father.

"That's right, Trace," Sonny said, touching his sleeve. "I just now learned that your father had been my informant all along. He was using me to draw your attention to Arthur's mismanagement of the company and to get you to do something about it. But what I don't understand," she said, addressing A.W., "is why you traded places with your brother. You *are* Trace Whittington, aren't you? The real Arthur IV's younger twin?"

"That's a lie!" Arthur V pointed an accusing finger at Sonny. "Why should we believe you? You're probably not even a real baroness."

"No, she isn't," A.W. said, standing barefooted and smiling knowingly at Sonny. "But in my book, she's pure nobility. She also happens to be telling the truth." He turned to his eldest son, who had collapsed in his chair. "I'm sorry, Arthur," Trace Whittington, Sr. said. "But thanks to Ms. Chapin, a new line of succession can finally be established at Whittington, Inc. One a man—or a woman—has to earn rather than merely be born into."

Trace passed Sonny, halting before his father. "If you're not who I'd always thought you were, who am I?"

Trace, Sr. looked into his son's eyes for some time before he spoke. "I could tell you that you're really *my* namesake and not your uncle's. But the truth is, Trace, you're your own man now."

Trace swallowed the lump forming in his throat. "But why did you do it? Why did you trade places with Uncle Arthur?"

Trace, Sr. took a deep breath. "From the time he was old enough to understand that he was expected to one day run Whittington, Inc., Arthur dreaded the prospect. I, on the other hand, never wanted to do anything else." He clamped a hand on Trace's shoulder. "Like you, son, I loved the business. I had hopes and dreams and plans for it, but also like you, I was the second son. No one would listen to me.

"So, when Arthur and I were fourteen," he said, addressing the rest of his family and the board, "we agreed to switch identities and swore a sacred oath never to reveal our pact. I couldn't ask the board to name you my successor on the grounds that a Trace Whittington had run the company for years without breaking my vow to my brother." Looking at Sonny, he winked. "Of course, if the baroness was smart enough to put two stars and my two feet together, I couldn't stop her."

Trace glanced away, shaking his head in amazement, then looked back at his father. "Now I know what you meant when you said you were glad I was still a gambling man. You wanted me to take your place because I, not Arthur, am your true namesake.''

The older man grabbed his son's broad shoulders and looked deeply into his eyes. "I wanted you to run the business because I knew from the time you were a boy, when you gave your all to keep up with me on those midnight swims, that you had what it took to run Whittington, Inc."

As Trace shared an embrace with his father, he felt he'd come home at last. Almost. No home of his could ever be complete without— "Sonny?" Turning and not finding her, he winnowed his way through the sea of back-slapping directors and stockholders who were going to make him the next chairman and CEO of Whittington Enterprises, Inc.

But that was no longer enough. He wanted to be the Man in Charge of Loving Sonny Chapin, and he wanted that job for the rest of his life. "Sonny!"

SONNY MADE HER WAY to her new desk, juggling a box filled with the contents of her old one at *Celebrity*. Under pressure from the publisher, Jack *had* fired her, but he'd been so relieved she'd bargained with Trace Whittington to drop the libel suit he'd authorized the charges she'd run up in Palm Beach. Then, claiming to be grateful she was now going to be the bane of some other poor overworked editor's life, he'd kissed her and wished her luck in her new job at the *Wall Street Journal*.

Her story on the rise, fall and rebirth of the Whittington empire under its new head, Trace Whittington II, which the paper had serialized, had won her a berth on the staff. She was going to like investigating the corporate and financial worlds, she decided as she set the box down next to her new computer. They weren't all that different from the circles she had covered as the baroness, cauldrons filled with stories of vanity, greed and subterfuge. Also, true heroism.

That was the other reason she was glad to be at the *Journal*. She felt she was sharing Trace's galaxy, even if her

orbit was far distant from his. She hadn't seen him since
the shareholders' meeting three weeks ago, when she'd left
him with his father, knowing he would be elected even
before the vote was taken. Knowing he had no more need
for her.

And by Millie's accounts, doing just fine, too. After his
election, his first official act was to appoint Brian to the
board and hire Millie as his executive secretary. He was
working day and night, getting up to speed, eliminating
bloat, jettisoning deadweight. Modernizing. He'd even
asked her father if he wanted to return to the presidency of
the company he had founded, but Edward Chapin was con-
tent on the mountain. He did recommend, however, that
Trace reinstate his old management team. Whittington
stock was on the rebound.

But not Sonny, not yet. Maybe not ever, she thought as
she removed the court summons he had returned to her
from among her belongings. Why was she still hanging on
to it? After all, Trace had dropped the suit, as he had promised.

"Excuse me."

Sonny looked up. A woman wearing a broad-shouldered
power suit walked toward her. An editor, a veep? "I'm
Sonny Chapin," she said, smiling and shaking the woman's
hand.

"Congratulations," the woman said, handing Sonny an
envelope.

"Thank you. I'm really glad to be…"

The woman walked away.

Sonny shrugged and opened the envelope. "Oh! What
does he expect me to do with these things—start a collection?" It was a new summons Trace had had served on her
citing her *Journal* stories, but there was nothing even remotely libelous in them, so what possible grounds could he
have for—

Seeing the summonses side by side, she noticed a startling difference. The one she had just received was for Sonora Chapin. But the one she had been served in Palm Beach was made out to "the Person or Persons professionally known as Baroness Sophia Oleska." If Trace had gone to Cara Mountain knowing she was the baroness and intending to seduce her, why hadn't he provided her legal name for the first summons? She recalled their last morning in Palm Beach when he had said, "I, Trace Whittington, had no idea that you, Sonny Chapin, were going to be served—"

Grabbing her bag, she dashed for the elevators.

"WHAT'S THE BIG IDEA, Whittington?"

As the doors to his office burst open, Trace turned from the window, genuinely surprised to see the subject of his fantasy charging toward him. "Sonny!"

"Don't play innocent with me," she said, slapping the summons on his desk. "What's the meaning of this?"

"Simple," he said, clasping his hands behind his back to keep them out of trouble. "We have a date in court."

"I'm not talking about the summons I got today, you double-crosser." Scooping up the paper, she rustled it in his face. "I'm talking about the one for the baroness."

Suddenly realizing where she was headed, Trace took the summons, crumpled it and tossed it in the trash. "It's meaningless. You know that."

"What *I* know is that *you* didn't know I was the baroness when we were on the mountain," she said, backing him to the window framing Manhattan's skyline. "You *did* fall in love with me there."

"Well, I certainly fell," Trace said, touching the temple he had bruised during their tumble down the mountain.

"You know what I mean," Sonny replied. "Why did you let me go on feeling deceived? Why didn't you ever tell me that Terry Wright had meant every word he said?"

Trace cocked a skeptical look at her. "In Palm Beach

you said you knew all along who I really was." Reversing course, he backed her into his desk. "If that was true, how could you possibly have felt deceived?"

"Well," Sonny stammered, trying to sidestep him and finding herself trapped.

"I...that is—"

"Sonny?" Trace pulled her into his arms. "The truth."

"Of course I knew who you really were," she said, crossing her fingers behind her back.

Trace released her. "Would you say that under oath in a court of law? Because I'm going to instruct my attorneys to ask you under cross-examination."

Pretzeling her arms, Sonny snorted. "That reminds me— what, pray tell, are you suing me over this time?"

"Your *Journal* stories of course."

"I know *that*," Sonny snapped. "What I don't know is why. They were the best pieces I've ever done."

"Oh, the writing was excellent," Trace said, shoving his hands into his pockets and circling behind her. "You're quite gifted. Still—" he scratched the back of his head "—there *were* some inaccuracies."

Sonny's eyes narrowed. "Such as..."

Trace leaned closer, inhaling the scent that used to start his days and haunt his nights. "To begin with, I thought you somewhat exaggerated your role in our escape from The Wall."

"The Wall?" Sonny turned, finding wisps of her hair clinging to his lips. She brushed them back. "Oh, you mean The Muscle."

"See, you didn't even get the poor man's name right," Trace said. Bearing down on her, he forced her into his chair and, clamping onto the armrests, caged her beneath him. "But not to worry. I'm sure we can work out a deal."

Sonny found Trace's closeness so overpowering, she could hardly breathe. "Something you want for something I want?"

"Exactly," he replied, cupping her cheek with his hand.

In a catlike motion Sonny rubbed her cheek against his palm. If she could have purred, she would have. "Would you like to give me a hint?"

"Uh-huh." Trace reclined the chair, sprawling Sonny beneath him. "With all the commotion at the stockholders meeting, it didn't hit me until two days ago that you called me—" he raised one knee onto the seat "—darling."

LYING IN A HAMMOCK beneath a blue Caribbean sky, Sonny recalled opening the medicine chest that morning and seeing a man's razor next to hers. With a groan of soul-deep satiety, she stretched her arms.

"Hey, watch it with that thing."

"Sorry," she said, turning on her side and admiring the brilliance encircling the third finger of her left hand. "I told my husband not to buy me such a big diamond."

Wrapping her in his arms, Trace lifted his wife on top of him. He ran his hands up her long delicious thighs, caressed her round naked bottom, got achingly hard at the feel of her bare breasts pressing against his chest. "I can see why he would want to lavish you with diamonds, madam," he said, plying her mouth with his own.

"Yes," she sighed, moving down his long taut body, trailing her tongue down his throat, over his nipples, giving them a bite. "He even arranged a honeymoon cruise on his sailing yacht. I can't imagine why he spoils me like that."

His hands spanning her waist, Trace lifted her toward him until her lips were where he wanted them, opposite his. Burying his hands in her lush hair, he drew her into a deep possessive kiss. "Because I love you, milady."

Closing her eyes, Sonny arched her neck, inviting him to nuzzle it. "I love you, too, whatever your name is."

Trace clasped her head between his hands, forcing her to look into his eyes. "Tell me the truth, Sonny. Up on

Cara Mountain, you didn't know who I *really* was, did you?"

Starting at his ear, she trailed kisses to his mouth, claimed it with her tongue and moaned when she felt his response against her inner thigh. "Maybe," she said, giving him a wicked grin.

"Maybe?" Trace rolled on top of her, tickling her sides. Sonny laughed, fighting his punishment. And neither of them heeded the violent rocking of the hammock.

They did, however, take note when it fell to the deck below.

Tangled in the netting and in each other, they laughed until they hurt.

"All right," Sonny said, snuggling against his side. "I confess I knew from the moment I fell into your arms who you really were."

Lifting his head, Trace looked down at her, dismayed. "You did?"

"Uh-huh," she said, propping her head on her hand and stroking her fingers over the face she adored. When she came to Trace's eyes, she stopped, noticing something new. Below the corner of his right eye, she saw a fine wrinkle. No, she corrected herself, it was a character line. Tenderly she kissed it. "You, my darling, were—and are—a man of conscience."

Harlequin Romance®

celebrates forty fabulous years!

Crack open the champagne and join us in celebrating Harlequin Romance's very special birthday.

Forty years of bringing you the best in romance fiction—and the best just keeps getting better!

Not only are we promising you three months of terrific books, authors and romance, but a chance to win a special hardbound 40th Anniversary collection featuring three of your favorite Harlequin Romance authors. And 150 lucky readers will receive an **autographed** collector's edition. Truly a one-of-a-kind keepsake.

Look in the back pages of any Harlequin Romance title, from April to June for more details.

Come join the party!

Look us up on-line at: http://www.romance.net

HR40THG2

Take 4 bestselling love stories FREE

Plus get a FREE surprise gift!

Special Limited-time Offer

Mail to Harlequin Reader Service®

3010 Walden Avenue
P.O. Box 1867
Buffalo, N.Y. 14240-1867

YES! Please send me 4 free Harlequin Love and Laughter™ novels and my free surprise gift. Then send me 4 brand-new novels every other month, which I will receive months before they appear in bookstores. Bill me at the low price of $2.90 each plus 25¢ delivery per book and applicable sales tax if any*. That's the complete price and a savings of over 10% off the cover prices—quite a bargain! I understand that accepting the books and gift places me under no obligation ever to buy any books. I can always return a shipment and cancel at any time. Even if I never buy another book from Harlequin, the 4 free books and the surprise gift are mine to keep forever.

102 BPA A7EF

Name	(PLEASE PRINT)
Address	Apt. No.
City	State	Zip

This offer is limited to one order per household and not valid to present Love and Laughter™ subscribers. *Terms and prices are subject to change without notice. Sales tax applicable in N.Y.

ULL-397   ©1996 Harlequin Enterprises Limited

And the Winner Is... You!

...when you pick up these great titles from our new promotion at your favorite retail outlet this June!

Diana Palmer
The Case of the Mesmerizing Boss

Betty Neels
The Convenient Wife

Annette Broadrick
Irresistible

Emma Darcy
A Wedding to Remember

Rachel Lee
Lost Warriors

Marie Ferrarella
Father Goose

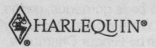

Free Gift Offer

With a Free Gift proof-of-purchase
from any Harlequin® book, you can receive
a beautiful cubic zirconia pendant.

This stunning marquise-shaped stone is a genuine cubic
zirconia—accented by an 18" gold tone necklace.
(Approximate retail value $19.95)

Send for yours today...
compliments of ⟨⟨HARLEQUIN®

To receive your free gift, a cubic zirconia pendant, send us one original proof-of-purchase, photocopies not accepted, from the back of any Harlequin Romance®, Harlequin Presents®, Harlequin Temptation®, Harlequin Superromance®, Harlequin Intrigue®, Harlequin American Romance®, or Harlequin Historicals® title available at your favorite retail outlet, together with the Free Gift Certificate, plus a check or money order for $1.65 U.S./$2.15 CAN. (do not send cash) to cover postage and handling, payable to Harlequin Free Gift Offer. We will send you the specified gift. Allow 6 to 8 weeks for delivery. Offer good until December 31, 1997, or while quantities last. Offer valid in the U.S. and Canada only.

Free Gift Certificate

Name: _____

Address: _____

City: _____ State/Province: _____ Zip/Postal Code: _____

Mail this certificate, one proof-of-purchase and a check or money order for postage and handling to: HARLEQUIN FREE GIFT OFFER 1997. In the U.S.: 3010 Walden Avenue, P.O. Box 9071, Buffalo NY 14269-9057. In Canada: P.O. Box 604, Fort Erie, Ontario L2Z 5X3.

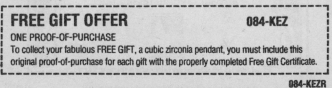

FREE GIFT OFFER   084-KEZ
ONE PROOF-OF-PURCHASE
To collect your fabulous FREE GIFT, a cubic zirconia pendant, you must include this original proof-of-purchase for each gift with the properly completed Free Gift Certificate.

084-KEZR

HE SAID

SHE SAID

Explore the mystery of male/female communication in this extraordinary new book from two of your favorite Harlequin authors.

Jasmine Cresswell and Margaret St. George bring you the exciting story of two romantic adversaries—each from their own point of view!

DEV'S STORY. CATHY'S STORY.
As he sees it. As she sees it.
Both sides of the story!

The heat is definitely on, and these two can't stay out of the kitchen!

Don't miss HE SAID, SHE SAID.
Available in July wherever Harlequin books are sold.

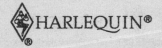

HESAID

LOVE & LAUGHTER™

MOTHER KNOWS BEST
—MAYBE!

These matchmaking moms have had
enough of their happy-to-be-single kids.
How is a respectable woman to become a
grandmother unless her offspring cooperates?
There's nothing to be done except to get
the kids down the aisle, even if they go
kicking and screaming all the way!

Plans are made, schemes hatched, plots
unraveled. Let the love and laughter begin!

#21 A MAN IN DEMAND
by Cheryl Anne Porter
June 1997

Watch for Kristine Rolofson's
Matchmaking Mom (from hell)
in September 1997.

Available wherever Harlequin books are sold.

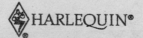

HARLEQUIN®